A PLACE IN TIME

by C. A. HOCKING

For Adam, Debra, Scott, Samuel
and Charlie

Also by C. A. HOCKING

DAMAGED GOODS
HOME TO ROOST
OLD FARTS ON A BUS
THE SARAH ANN ELLIOTT SERIES
THE AUNT EDNA STORIES

CHAPTER ONE

"Enough!" The word exploded above Dan with an impact that jerked him awake. Patricia Campbell stood over her husband and screamed the word again.

Shocked, Dan rolled onto his back and looked up at her, squinting against the harsh ceiling light behind her that cast her face into a shadowed mask of fury, despair and a love pushed to its limits of patience and forgiveness. She was shaking, her hands clenched as if she wanted to raise them against him.

He pulled himself up on the pillows and reached out to calm her. She jumped back as if he had been about to hit her. "Trish, love, what's wrong?"

"What's wrong? Everything! Everything's wrong, Dan, every damn thing I can think of is wrong. You're wrong, I'm wrong, the boys are wrong, your mother is wrong. And I've had enough, do you hear, I've had enough!" Her face twisted, her mouth trembled and she exploded into loud, miserable tears.

He swung his legs over the side of the bed. Angus and Hamish were standing in the doorway behind her, their faces registering shocked disbelief at hearing their gentle mother's outburst. He noticed blue bruising down the left side of Hamish's face and the beginning of a black eye. Angus's shirt was torn across one shoulder.

Footsteps coming up the stairs heralded Connie's entrance, short grey hair framing her sweet, concerned

1

face. She placed herself between her grandsons, her arms instinctively wrapping around their waists. Both boys towered over her. "What's wrong?"

Trish turned. "Everything!"

"Come on, boys," Connie said quietly, "this is between your Mum and Dad." She began to guide the boys away, but Trish cried out, "Stay! You're part of this. All of you. Stay!"

Dan started to raise himself off the bed, but Trish jerked forward and thrust him back onto the pillows in an aggressive manner completely out of character. He stayed where he landed, unsure of what was coming next. Trish stepped closer to the bed and took a shuddering breath.

"Dan Campbell," she began angrily, tears still streaming unchecked down her face, "in eighteen years of marriage, we've not had a cross word between us. I love you dearly." She leaned forward and her energy loomed over him. "Never doubt that, but I can't take this anymore. Every year, your birthday comes around and you take to your bed for a month. We've tried to understand, we've tried to help and we all make the best of it, but today that stops."

He opened his mouth to ask her what she meant, but Trish hadn't finished. "Other families go out to dinner and buy presents and have a cake with candles or maybe even go on a holiday, but not us. Oh no, we creep around the house because you can't handle any noise. We mustn't disturb you, poor Dan is having a bad time. Eleven months of the year, you are the best husband, father and son," she glanced briefly towards her sons and mother-in-law, "anyone in this world could want, but for a month

2

you are a stranger to us all. We can't talk to you because you aren't here. You're," she waved a hand towards the window, "out there, somewhere else, some place we can't go. Except for Connie, she knows where you are, but she doesn't say anything except that she mustn't interfere, she mustn't influence you in any way."

Trish wiped tears from her cheeks with the sleeve of her blouse. "Well, what does that mean, Dan, what exactly does that mean? How can it be interfering to help you, to talk to you?" She looked back at Connie. "Why won't the two of you talk about it?"

Connie, her face unreadable, didn't reply.

Trish raised her hands in a gesture of despair. "See what I mean? How do you expect us to cope if the two of you won't be open about what happened? Wouldn't it help if you talked about it? But, no, the only two people in the world who could explain this annual descent into depression won't share it with us, and that leaves me and the boys in the dark." With a deep shuddering breath, she tried to calm herself a little. "All we know is that your father was murdered on your eleventh birthday and they never caught the killer. We know you witnessed it, but you've had years and years of counselling and still you go to ground every birthday. It's got to stop."

Connie stepped between the boys as if to go to Trish to comfort her, but Trish unexpectedly swung around and held her hand up to stop her. The shock in Connie's face was tangible, but she stepped back.

Connie had always taken great care not to meddle in her son's marriage. She loved Trish as the daughter she'd never had and the two women had always shared a close relationship, but this distraught person before her now was something new, something none of them had ever seen before.

Connie looked quickly at her son, the unkempt hair and unshaven face, the confusion and distress, and a sharp memory suddenly appeared before her. She stared at him for a second longer, then dropped her eyes, her face flushing with the shock of what this moment might mean. She'd wondered for thirty years if it would ever really happen.

Trish suddenly pointed to Connie and shouted, "There! There in your face, that look! I've seen it before, as if there is something you know about all this that nobody else does. It's like there's a conspiracy between the two of you to shut me out as if I'm some sort of outsider. Do you know what that has been like for me all these years? I love you, Connie, love you like my own mother, and I've tried to understand, truly I have, but," she turned back to Dan, "today ..." she took another deep breath to steady herself, "... today your own son was beaten up because of you."

Dan looked at Hamish's injured face, then saw the bloodied, grazed hands and torn clothes. "What happened?"

"He was teased at school because of you and he went to your defence. Six lads, Dan. He fought six big lads because they said his father was a loon. They punched him and knocked him to the ground and kicked him. Our own Hamish, who has never given us a moment's worry in his sixteen years. Angus saw his brother in trouble and went to his aid. It would have been much worse if a teacher hadn't intervened, but now they are both on suspension for fighting, the exams are in three

4

weeks and my babies are hurting. And all because of you, Dan, all because of you."

Trish took a step back, folded her arms across her chest and waited. She was finished.

They were all frozen in the shock of the moment, paralysed by the first real crisis they had known as a family. Dan looked up and said, "Trish … Hamish ... I'm so sorry ... I don't know … what do you want me to do?"

Trish, suddenly feeling drained from the outburst, flopped onto the bed next to Dan and said with a pinched mouth, "I want you to tell us what it is that happens inside your head, what it is that happened to you when your father died. I'm not moving from this bed until you do and I want all of us to hear it."

Dan stared at her, taking in slowly just what it was she was asking of him. He glanced at his mother, but she had that "I mustn't interfere, I mustn't influence" look on her face, just as Trish had noted. He knew that look so well and had wondered more than once why it was that she felt it was so important that she keep an emotional distance when it came to the subject of his father's death. Surely it might have helped him if she would only open up and talk about it? After all, she had witnessed it too. All the counselling in the world was nothing compared to the healing that might begin if he could talk to the only other person who knew, who understood. She'd shut him out for some reason. Her silence was a mystery to him. As his silence was a mystery to Trish.

Suddenly, he understood exactly how Trish was feeling. He pulled her into an embrace and felt her sag against his chest. "I don't know if I can," he said simply.

"I don't understand some of it myself. Some of it doesn't make sense, but I don't know why."

"Try, Dan, please. We can't go on like this. You have to try."

He felt the helplessness in her words. How could he have been so blind to the toll his behaviour had taken on his nearest and dearest? He looked up at his sons and wondered what they thought of their father at this moment. Trish was right, he had to try.

"Alright, I'll do my best, but it won't be easy listening. It's an ugly story."

"We can handle it, Dad," Angus said with the bravado of a fourteen year old. "We just want you to get better."

Hamish stepped forward. "We'll help you, Dad." His lip trembled. This had been a bad day for him.

Connie said quietly, "Terry is downstairs. He can take care of the bar for a while. He won't mind." She closed the bedroom door behind her. "We won't be disturbed."

They arranged themselves around the bedroom silently, preparing themselves for whatever it was they were about to hear.

Dan leaned against the bedhead and closed his eyes briefly. Where to begin? Well, there was one obvious place. He opened his eyes and looked up at them. "Alright. It was my eleventh birthday."

He inhaled deeply. They waited. He began slowly.

"I'd been out with Dad all morning looking for rabbits and foxes. Dad had a rifle – he called it the elephant gun because it was so powerful – and he let me use it when we went out shooting, but the recoil used to knock me off my feet. He'd promised me a rifle of my own for my birthday and was teasing me about it, saying I was too

6

young and that if I couldn't handle the elephant gun, then I shouldn't have a rifle of my own yet. So I was trying hard to manage his rifle, to prove to him that I was ready for one of my own. He used to say, Come on boy, let's go kill some elephants, but all we ever came back with was a few mangled rabbits for the stew pot. I was still young enough to think there might be an elephant out there somewhere."

Dan paused, remembering. "It was always exciting with Dad. We had a farm in Australia back then, boys, but you already know that. New South Wales. How many acres, Mum - fifty thousand?"

Connie nodded, her eyes cast down almost as if she wasn't listening, but he sensed she was listening intently.

Dan continued. "Sounds like a lot to you boys, living here in England with villages and towns every few miles, but it was by no means the biggest property in the district and the nearest town was over an hour's drive away. Wheat and sheep. I still remember thousands of sheep in the holding paddock, waiting to be shorn. Merinos. I believe our property had a reputation for producing fine wool. The farm used to belong to my grandparents and their parents before them. My grandmother died before I was born and my grandfather when I was a baby, so I never knew them. My grandmother was from Sussex, from this very village and met my grandfather as a young man when he was travelling around Britain. She went back to Australia with him. My great-grandfather built the farmhouse himself, a big sandstone place with high ceilings, polished floors and beautifully carved fireplaces. I have wonderful memories of that house. Dad was a farm hand to begin with, he worked for my grandparents. That's how he met Mum - your Gran."

He saw Connie's eyes flicker and her hands clench around the tea cup. "Mum, if this is too much for you ..."

She said without looking up, "Don't you worry about me, I'm fine."

"Sure? OK. So. It was my eleventh birthday." He spoke quietly, carefully, trying to choose his words to paint a picture of this memory for Trish and his sons.

"We'd come back just before lunch and discovered that one of the sheepdogs had produced a litter of puppies. Mum bred champion sheepdogs back then and had already promised the first five puppies to local farmers, but had said that if there were more than five puppies, then I could keep one. Well, we discovered six puppies and I was beside myself with excitement. I'd never had a dog of my own before. Our dogs were working dogs, not pets, so it was a big event for me." Dan smiled a little at the sweet memory. "We called her Lucky Six, Lucky for short, didn't we, Mum?"

Connie nodded briefly.

"I still had Lucky when I met Trish at uni. Poor old Lucky, she was old and arthritic by then and we lost her before you boys came along. She was very important to me because ... well, I guess she was the last link with Dad. The last connection with a happy childhood that ended later that very day. You see, she was born the day he died."

Dan shook his head sadly. "Anyway, where was I? We'd come back to the house and I took Lucky to show your Gran. She had made me a birthday cake and we were waiting on the veranda for it to cool. Then Gran saw the stranger standing next to the house-paddock gate. He was just standing there, staring at us. Gran walked over to him and they came back together. She said the stranger's car had run out of petrol on the main road and Dad would need to drive the man back with a jerrycan of petrol, but the man said not to bother. He'd walk back and leave the empty jerrycan by the main gate. I remember thinking he was crazy not to let Dad drive him back, it was such a long way, but he insisted. Then Dad started quizzing the man. I don't think he liked him for some reason. He was a bit snappy, but he said he'd help him."

"Dad went to get the petrol from the shed and Gran asked the man to stay for lunch and a piece of birthday cake before he left." Dan paused, uncertain about something. "He sat next to me, but for the life of me, I can't remember his face. I remember he had a funny accent. Mum, didn't you ask him about that accent?"

"I did," she answered quietly. "I thought he sounded a little like my mother. She was English of course. But he said he'd been born in Australia."

Dan stared at his mother. "You've never told me that before, Mum."

"No," she said simply, offering nothing further. Dan felt the frustration rise up in him, but continued anyway.

"Well, I don't remember a lot about the man while he was at lunch because I had other things to think about. Your Gran gave me a camera and Dad finally gave me my own rifle and, what with Lucky, the camera and the new rifle, I was so excited I could hardly contain myself. What I do remember is that when Dad came back with the petrol, I could see he was cross about something. I don't think he was happy about the stranger staying for lunch for some reason. Anyway, I went off to do something and when I came back, the stranger was gone and Dad was inside. He told me to go and play. Gran was inside with him, cleaning up I suppose. I don't remember too much about the rest of the afternoon. I spent it with the puppy, mostly taking photographs. Tea came and went and then I was in bed." He stopped and looked around him uncertainly, as if needing a distraction.

Trish moved a little closer and looked up at him. "Don't stop, Dan. Just say it, one word at a time. Take however long you need, but don't stop."

He nodded. Psychiatrists, psychologists and counsellors had said much the same to him at this point in the story over the years, but it was here that the telling took on a black dreamlike quality and the story became a nightmare.

"I don't know how long I'd been asleep, but I was woken by a noise, a loud noise. I still don't know if the noise was something breaking or something crashing, but it was very loud and woke me with a fright. I tried to get out of bed, but I felt heavy and couldn't move my arms or legs properly. Then I heard loud voices, but I couldn't tell where they came from, inside or outside, they sounded like they were all around me. I tried to get out of bed again, but it felt as if I was being held down. I was very frightened. I managed to sit up, but when I tried to move, I fell out of bed. It took me by surprise, even more than the noises. I pulled myself up onto my feet and started to walk towards the kitchen, but I was all weak and soft and needed to lean against the wall. The passage seemed long and dark, but I could see the glow of the kitchen light at the end of it. It looked so far away. I wanted to call out to Mum and Dad, but I couldn't get any sound out. I just couldn't move properly. It was almost like being under water, except that the water had turned to jelly and I had to fight my way through it. Everything looked strange, the colours, it all kept moving. I don't know. I don't understand." He shook his head, then continued. "The sounds - I could tell now that they were coming from the kitchen, but they were warped and sort of slow. It seemed to take forever to reach the kitchen. Then ..."

Dan suddenly didn't want to go on, despite the encouraging faces around him. He closed his eyes to shut out their need.

Connie reached across and took his hand in hers. There were tears in her eyes and her hand was clammy.

Dan opened his eyes and looked down at his large hand entwined in his mother's small hand. The words came in a whisper. "I saw you, Mum, fighting with the stranger, trying to push him away. He had his back to me, but I could see your face. It was all messed up and bloody. It was such a shock. I think I looked away, but it was like everything was in slow motion. Then ... then I saw Dad. He was on the other side of the kitchen, slumped against the wall and ..." He gulped and felt Connie's hand tighten around his. "... he had no face. There was blood everywhere. The kitchen was red with blood. I felt like I was drowning in blood. I couldn't breathe. I couldn't move."

The terror and heartache of it all gushed through him and he began to shake.

Trish, ashen faced, said softly, "Jesus."

Hamish and Angus were wide eyed and motionless, too afraid to speak.

Connie's tears spilled down her face. She squeezed her son's hand hard and said fearfully, "Go on, dearest, go on."

Dan forced the words from a throat that threatened to close on him. "It seemed to take a moment for me to put it all together. My Dad was dead and the stranger who'd killed him was standing there with my Mum and I knew he was going to kill her, too. I had to stop him, but I didn't know what to do. I tried to move forward and felt something at my feet. I looked down and saw my new rifle on the floor. Then I saw Dad's rifle by the fridge. It had blood on it and I knew instantly that the stranger had used it to kill Dad. I remember thinking he was going to use my rifle to kill Mum and she was trying to stop him. And then it was like everything around me stopped, like it all froze. I reached down for my rifle. I didn't know if it was loaded, but the safety was off. I felt sick and dizzy. There was a strange sort of mumbling sound in the room, like someone was talking in the background. It was all so confusing. I brought the rifle up to fire. I remember thinking, don't miss, don't miss. I pulled the trigger, I heard the shot, but I don't remember another thing until I woke up in hospital the next day. At first I thought I was still in the kitchen and I couldn't stop screaming. Then you came to me, Mum."

Dan leaned across and kissed his mother's hand. "You had bandages around your head and your arm, and your face was bruised and swollen. I kept asking you where Dad was. You didn't want to tell me at first, but I kept asking and then you told me Dad was dead.

The stranger had shot him and then escaped. The police were out looking for him. You told me that I'd shot the stranger and that was what made him run away. You said that the bullet I fired had passed through his arm and into yours, that you'd had an operation during the night to fix your arm and that you were alright. You said that I'd saved you, that I was very brave."

Dan looked at his mother. "But I wasn't brave, Mum, I was afraid. If I had been really brave, I would have saved Dad. I would have run up to the kitchen at the first noise, but I was so afraid, I could hardly move. If I'd woken up when the stranger first came to the house that night, I'd have had time to get Dad's rifle and I could have saved him." Suddenly, his face twisted into an ugly mask. "And the stranger is still out there somewhere, living his life while Dad has been dead these thirty years. I feel his presence in the world and I want to get him. I want to kill him!"

The venom in Dan's voice shocked them all. Connie looked away, her face white and strained.

Trish said gently, "Is that what torments you the most, Dan?"

"Yes. But there's something else." He gave them all a baffled look. "Something I've been trying to understand since it happened. It's as if ... as if there is something wrong with the memory itself."

"What do you mean?"

"I'm not sure I can explain it. I've gone over it a million times. I dream about it, I've talked endlessly about it with different counsellors over the years, but still ..." Dan paused, searching his memory for an answer.

"... but still?" Hamish prompted.

"… but still I can't quite pinpoint what's wrong, as if I'm missing something. Something that would put the last piece in the puzzle. I've always felt that if I could do that, then we could find the killer, give the whole episode some closure. For me and for your grandmother."

Hamish asked, "Did the police know who he was, Dad? The stranger?"

"No," Dan replied slowly, "he was a clever bastard. He ran off after I shot him, but the police believed he stayed close to the house, because after Gran got us in the car and left for the hospital, he went back and cleaned up all traces of himself. There wasn't much left for the police to use in their search for him. A pair of shoe prints, if I remember, but they weren't any help in finding him."

"Why didn't Gran ring for the police or an ambulance?"

"There were no phone lines out there then, Hamish, and it was long before satellite phones. We were quite isolated, which I suppose made it much easier for the stranger to do what he did."

"He must have left something behind," Angus said. "Blood, fingerprints, DNA?"

"There was no DNA around in those days. The police were very thorough, but even so, they found no fingerprints or blood belonging to a stranger. A couple of years ago, your Gran got a letter from the police in Sydney saying that they were having another look at the case, including DNA tests from evidence kept since that time. You know, clothing and blood. The police here arranged for our DNA to be taken and sent off to Australia. We got a report later saying that they'd found our DNA, but nothing from a third person. The report also said they believe the evidence had been corrupted in some way over the years, rendering useless what they had kept. Something about the shoe prints being mixed up somehow."

"But you shot him. There must have been blood?"

"No, not even a trace of his blood, Angus. The bastard was smart, very smart. He was thorough when he went back to clean up."

"So what was his motive?" Hamish asked, he and Angus being devotees of all the current television crime shows.

Dan looked at his sons, his dear, clever, secure sons. They were no longer children, they were young men. He thought they were old enough to hear the truth.

"The police believed he was after Gran, that he intended to harm her."

"You mean rape?" Angus said in a startled voice.

Connie raised her eyes slowly and looked around at all of them. "That's what the police said at the time," she replied woodenly.

Trish leaned forward and laid her head against her husband's chest. His heart was beating rapidly. "You were just a little boy, Dan. What you did was remarkable and probably saved your mother's life and your own. It would have been a lot worse if you hadn't intervened. Wouldn't you agree, Connie?"

Something flashed across Connie's features, her mouth twitching briefly at the corners. "That I can agree with absolutely, Patricia. Without a doubt, Dan saved both our lives."

Trish looked up at Dan's face, reading him perfectly. "But knowing that is not enough, is it Dan? It won't give you the peace you need so badly. Didn't that last psychiatrist tell you that you should go back to the farm to confront your memories? Didn't she say that was what you needed to do?"

"Yes, but ..."

"But you said you were too busy and you couldn't afford to make the trip. That was three years ago when we were still paying off the renovations to the pub. We can afford it now and you can certainly take the time off. I think you should do it. I think you should do it without delay. It's your birthday in three days, you could be there by then."

"Yes, Dad."

"That would be good, Dad."

There was a knock on the door. Terry, tall, grey and handsome, came in, his face concerned. "Everything alright here?" He bent down to kiss Connie and reached for her hand.

Dan looked up at his stepfather uncertainly. "Bit of a crisis happening here, Terry. Sorry."

"That's OK, Dan. What's up?"

Connie explained briefly, then said, "Dan and Patricia need to make a trip to Australia. You and I can take care of the pub..."

"Oh, no," Trish interrupted, "I can't go. The boys have exams in three weeks and I need to be here for that. I can get what they need from the school before the exams and help them with it at home. They may be suspended, but they can still go back to take those exams and I won't allow them to be disadvantaged by this, not after all the work they've done. I can't go."

Terry was looking at Connie and an understanding passed between them. "You should go, Connie. Trish and I can manage here, and the boys will chip in. These are your memories, too. Perhaps you need this as much as Dan."

Connie gave Dan a penetrating look and asked, "What do you think, Dan?"

"Of course you should come, Mum. I don't think I can do it without you."

"Are you quite sure this is what you want to do?"

"I don't know if I want to do it, Mum, but considering what has happened to Hamish and Angus today, I think I must. Maybe it will help, I don't know, but Trish is right. I have to do something about this. The way I feel as each birthday comes around, it's hell. And I've been so selfish about this ..."

"No, Dad, you haven't been selfish," Hamish interjected in his thoughtful way. "If I'd seen some stranger come into the house and kill you and threaten Mum, I'd be feeling a bit screwed up, too. And if I was feeling like the memory of it wasn't quite right, I'd be wanting to go back to see if I could straighten things out."

"Me too," Angus said, then added, "And you're no loon, Dad, we know that."

Dan smiled. Looking around at his family, he knew he was a lucky man, luckier than most. He wanted for nothing here. He owed it to them to find closure and move on.

Connie was still watching him closely. She said suddenly, "It may not be as you thought, Danny. When you go back. You may find things back there that ... disturb you."

"What do you mean, Mum? What could be more disturbing than what actually happened?"

Connie blinked and looked around. "Nothing," she said, "nothing at all. I was just meaning that, well, things change after thirty years. It may not be what you expect." Even as she said it, Dan instinctively knew she wasn't telling him what she had really meant, and wondered again what went on inside her mind. To all outward appearances, she was a placid, quietly spoken and very content woman, but after what she had been through, surely some place in her mind had been deeply affected by the murder of her first husband. Surely some corner of her memory revisited the horror of that day from time to time, as did his.

Trish said, "Of course it will look different, Dan. Nothing stays the same. Goodness, when I went to my high school reunion last year, I couldn't even find the street where the school was. Everything changes."

She rose quickly and began to organise them all. "So, that's settled. Dan, you and Connie pack, I'll get started on the dinner. Terry, you'd better get downstairs or they'll be thinking the drinks are free. Hamish dear, can you and Angus get on the internet and look for some good flights to Sydney. And a hire car to drive from there to the town. Dad will tell you what it's called. I'll get your shorts and cotton shirts out of the back cupboard, Dan. It'll be spring over there, won't it? That'll be nice. A bit of sun will do you good, both of you. Come on, hop to it everyone, the sooner we do this and get it behind us, the sooner we can all get on with our lives."

18

CHAPTER TWO

"Trish was right," Connie said as they unpacked a few things in the upstairs room of the hotel. "Everything has changed. This place was jumping with life when I was growing up here. The bar downstairs was always full and visitors sometimes couldn't get a room because there were so many people passing through the town. That was before they built the freeway and the bypass missed the town by ten miles."

She hung clothing in an old wardrobe. "And there were three other pubs like this one back then. Now, this is all that's left and it looks shabby and almost deserted. The only person I've seen that I know is Irene. We were at school here together, although she tells me that the school closed down ten years ago. The drought on top of everything else, I suppose, so many people moved away. Her father owned this pub then and now she owns it, but I wouldn't have recognised her if she hadn't introduced herself."

Connie closed the wardrobe door and opened a drawer. "She told me our farm has had several owners since we left, but the last owners lost everything with this drought. She went out there a couple of years ago, said the house had practically fallen down and the last owners had cut down all the trees on the property to sell for timber to try to keep things afloat for as long as they could, but like so many others, they had to leave in the end. She said it was like a desert out there now, no trees, just a dustbowl. Even the bores had dried up. She said I won't recognise the place." She shook her head sadly. "Who would have thought? It was such a prosperous property for so many years. I'm glad we left when we did."

"Does she remember Dad and what happened?" Dan asked, having already deposited his luggage in the room next door.

"Oh yes, she remembers well enough. He was a local lad, we all knew each other back then. She asked me if I'd married again in England. I told her I had and that, like her, I was also an innkeeper these days. She wanted to know if I was happy."

"That was nice of her to ask," Dan said idly, his mind on the drive out to the farm. "When do you want to leave? Early tomorrow?"

Connie stopped unpacking and turned to face him, giving him another of her unfathomable looks. "Early tomorrow would be fine," she said calmly, although Dan sensed a certain tension behind the words. "Irene said that the road is sealed all the way out there now, but it still takes about an hour. I don't think we'll want to linger. The way she described the farm as it is, I think it will depress me to see it. We could be back here for lunch."

"Sounds like you did well to sell when you did, Mum. Was that a hard decision at the time?"

"No," she said with that unnatural calmness again, "I was advised to sell and it proved to be good advice."

"I'm glad you did. I can't imagine living here now. It seems so ... so empty, so brown and barren."

Connie smiled. "You've become used to lush green England. I suppose I have, too. Come on, dearest, let's go downstairs and join Irene. She said she'd have a cold beer ready for us both. I'd forgotten how hot it gets out here. A cold beer sounds just right."

The evening was spent in pleasant reminiscence with Irene and after Dan kissed his mother goodnight and retired to his room, he lay in bed and thought about that unnatural calmness of his mother's whenever the subject of Dad came up.

For some years after they left Australia and he was struggling to adjust to a new country, new accents, new school, new expectations, he would sometimes say to his mother, "Do you remember that great time when Dad took me spotlighting (or yabbying in the dam or rabbit trapping or shooting etc etc)," and she would always answer with that calmness, "Yes, I remember." Then she married Terry and it was his stepfather who took him fishing, hiking, cycling and helped him with his homework.

It was Terry who guided him into computers and the career that supported them all while they built up the village pub that Connie had inherited on her aunt's death. Terry had become a beloved stand-in father, but still Dan would lie in bed at night and remember those sweet days with his Dad, those days of warmth and light and laughter.

Suddenly, Dan could see what might be bothering his mother now. She'd come back to Australia with him, but not for any need of her own. She'd come back because he needed to come back.

Connie was a very gentle, patient woman and he'd never seen her lose her temper, not even once. She was, by nature, almost compliant, her own needs always subjugated to the needs of her family, and it occurred to him that Terry had never once taken advantage of that. He was also gentle and intelligent, a good match for Connie. He'd been kind, generous and respectful to them both since they first met him when he'd started as the school principal in the village. He'd come into the pub to ask for a room while he looked for somewhere to live, but he never moved out. In fact, they'd been inseparable since that first meeting, and Dan wondered why he had dragged her away from the man she so clearly adored.

Now he was planning to take her out to the farm tomorrow and dredge up all the old pain and sorrow that she must have experienced thirty years ago, just so he could put his own pain and sorrow into focus, deal with it and hopefully move on. He berated himself for such selfishness. No, he mustn't put her through that. He had no right. She had dealt with her experiences and memories in her own way, and so must he. He'd tell her in the morning that he'd go alone.

His mind was going at a thousand miles an hour and he couldn't settle. He got up and took a couple of sleeping pills, hoping his mother had done the same. Back in bed, he tried to imagine what the house might look like now. Irene had said it was a sad echo of what it once was.

Dan's great-grandmother had planted a large garden and he remembered tall trees, scented roses and a big vegetable patch. His English grandmother had added a herb garden and a fishpond and he remembered dangling his feet in the pond on hot days. Mum had put her own touch to the garden with white daisies and more roses. She used to point out which plants and trees had been planted by which Campbell wife. Now he tried to imagine the house in ruins with the garden dead. It was not an easy vision to conjure up, but he didn't want to be unrealistic about his expectations.

And what would he do when he got there? Maybe walk around the house paddock with the high chicken-wire fence that had been built to keep the rabbits out of the garden, and meander through whatever remained of the orchard, then wander around the sheds and the house. Perhaps sit on the front veranda and work through his memories, try to put them into the perspective of the adult he now was, with thirty years between the present and the past, or perhaps he'd sit on the back veranda and gaze across paddocks that had once looked like a golden ocean just before harvest with the hazy blue hills in the distance.

As sleep filtered into his thoughts, he suddenly remembered the taste of the rainwater from the tank behind the big shed, the tank that was always shaded and cool. Sweet water with a slight metallic bite, more refreshing than anything he'd ever experienced since. He could taste it now, right now, as if he'd just taken a gulp. He kicked his boots off and ran a little of the water over his hot sweaty feet, knowing he'd get a telling off if Mum saw him wasting water like that, but also knowing Dad wouldn't mind as it was Dad who showed him how to do it.

Dad didn't worry about things like that. Dad was easy going, a joker with a loud laugh who would catch him up and throw him onto his shoulders and carry him across to the house at a run. "Come on, boy," he'd shout, "let's go see what your Mum's got us for tea!" He'd drop young Danny with a thud at the kitchen door, pull a bottle of beer from the fridge and state, "It's too bloody hot in here! We'll have tea on the veranda."

Mum would be at the sink with her back to them, quiet, always quiet. She'd collect the tea things from the kitchen table and follow them out to the veranda, reminding Danny to wash his hands before eating. Danny would run to the bathroom and back again, for he was hungry. Hungry like a man, like his Dad.

Mum would be hurrying to get tea on the veranda table because Dad didn't like to wait. He'd say, "Come on, Con, what's a man gotta do to get fed around here?" Mum would rush so much that some times she dropped things or even broke things.

Dad would laugh and as tea progressed, he laughed louder and louder, and Danny laughed right along with him. Dad laughing, that's what Dan remembered most, Dad laughing louder and louder ....

He slept.

CHAPTER THREE

Connie was waiting for Dan downstairs in the dining room, a pot of tea on the table and the breakfast menu in her hand. Even with the air-conditioning, there was a feeling of gritty heat in the room. She wore a loose chambray shirt and knee length shorts with leather sandals, a look he hadn't seen on her since they'd left Australia. Her short grey hair was still wet from the shower and her face was free of make-up. Apart from the grey hair, she looked more like he remembered her when he was a boy than in all their years in England. She'd be sixty next year, but today she looked closer to fifty. The dry heat and casual country look seemed to suit her.

She rose to greet him with the familiar morning kiss on the cheek and began to pour him a cup of tea. As he took his seat opposite her, he said quickly, apologetically, "Mum, I think I'll go out there by myself today, if you don't mind."

He was aware the tea was no longer pouring from the pot. He looked up. Connie, her face suddenly pale, was holding the pot as if frozen, her eyes downcast. He took the pot from her. She sat down slowly, carefully, almost as if she was in pain. Her hands were trembling.

"It's alright with you, isn't it, Mum? I mean, if you really want to come, of course, you should. It's just that, well, I thought it might be a bit rough on you."

She looked up. "Are you sure?" was all she said, but once again he felt the mystery of unexplained meaning behind her words.

Dan looked into his mother's face, but she looked away. "Mum?" he said, confused, then "Mum?" again. She brought her gaze slowly to his. Were her eyes damp? He couldn't be sure. "Mum, what are you thinking? I can never tell."

She stared at him for a second, just a second, that's all it was, but he saw that 'thing' cross her face, that mysterious thing that always left him feeling that words were being left unsaid. Important words. She saw his thoughts and said in a rush, "We'll talk about it when you get back. We'll talk about everything then. I promise."

"Why can't we talk about it now, Mum? What's wrong with now?"

Instead of answering the question, she was staring at his shirt. "I haven't seen that shirt before," she said. He looked down. It was one that Trish had bought for him, a black and white check with a distinctive red thread running through the fabric.

"No, it's new. Trish bought it for me last time she was in London."

Connie's gaze seemed riveted to the shirt. After a moment, she looked up at him, looked at him as if she was seeing him for the first time, her gaze following the lines of his face, his hair, his neck and again down to his shirt. She leaned forward and rested her hand on his watch. "This is new, too?"

"You remember this. The boys gave it to me for my 40th last year."

"Yes. I remember now. It's just that I hadn't taken much notice of it before." She leaned a little to the side and peered down at his shoes under the table, then looked up again at his face. She was trembling.

Dan's heart contracted. He shouldn't have brought her, there were too many bad memories. He squeezed her hand reassuringly. "Mum, what is it?"

Connie gave him a strangely desperate look, something he couldn't begin to interpret, and said gently, "I've always loved you, Danny. You've come first in every way. Always."

"I know that, Mum, I've always known that. And I love you, too. Look, please don't worry, I'll be fine out there on my own. And maybe we can go out there together tomorrow after I've had time to think things through today. I'm sure that my head will clear once I've had a bit of a walk around the farm. You know, some quiet time to just let it happen."

Connie nodded. "I'll wait here for you."

The waitress arrived, cutting their conversation short. They ordered and talked about what he should take with him and what she would do to pass the time until his return. "I'll be back by lunchtime," he said.

"It may take longer than you think. Take something to snack on, like some biscuits or snack bars, and plenty of water. It's a long drive out there and back."

"Already thought of that," he smiled at her.

After breakfast, Dan collected a few provisions from Irene and packed them into a cooler in the back of the four-wheel drive. Connie and Irene waved to him from the hotel veranda. Irene was delighted that Connie was staying behind and was busily arranging for a few old school friends who still lived in the town to come to morning tea for a reunion. Dan hoped that would keep Mum's mind occupied. He didn't want to be worrying about her today. He'd have enough to deal with as it was.

The trip west from town was depressing. Dan remembered this time of year as having been full of energy and life, with green paddocks, vigorous crops, sheep and lambs, lively markets, prosperous homesteads and busy people.

Now, he passed properties that were deserted, derelict or so run down that the struggle for the farmers who managed to cling to their barren land was tangible in their dirty, aging vehicles, shabby homesteads and bare paddocks. No stock was to be seen anywhere. He knew the district had experienced droughts before, but this one had brought the area to its knees.

He was grateful that Mum had sold up the year after Dad's death when things were still prosperous and she could get a good price. The Taylors had bought the property first, he remembered now. They had been neighbours, good neighbours who, along with other good neighbours, had helped Mum bring in the crop that terrible year, helped with the shearing and the fencing and never asked for anything in return. When the Taylors saw the struggle Mum was having, they'd made her an offer she'd accepted without question. At the same time, Mum's aunt in England had asked them to move in with her and help run the inn. It had worked out well for them all.

Dan turned into the road that ran past the farm. Another fifteen minutes and he'd be there. He looked for familiar landmarks - two homesteads on the right with the school bus stop between them, the big place on the left set far back from the road behind tall pine trees, the windmill that clattered constantly in the breeze, the holding yards where sheep were loaded onto trucks. He found them, or what remained of them, in the hazy brown heat, but most of his attention was taken up with the poor condition of the road. It hadn't been upgraded in years and manoeuvring around deep potholes took considerable concentration. He had almost driven past the farm before he realised where he was.

The two wide stone pillars which had served as gate posts were still standing, although they were both missing their flat tops and looked like jagged broken teeth. They had once supported an ornate timber sign saying 'CAMPBELL', but there was nothing left of that now. The gate between the pillars had buckled and twisted away from the rusted hinges. Dan turned the car towards the entrance, then braked hard. The cattle grid was gone. Even the four wheel drive would not get across the deep gaping hole before him.

He looked around and took stock. The post and barbed-wire fences that stretched for miles on either side of the farm entrance were in a bad state of disrepair, but still intact enough to stop him from driving through. He thought about cutting the barbed wire, but quickly realised he didn't have the tools for it. Besides, there was something innately wrong about cutting someone's fences, even if they had once been your own. The country boy with country principles still lingered inside him.

Dan got out of the car and surveyed the situation. He could turn around and go back, but he didn't want to. He was here now. He wanted to get it over with and get home to Trish and the boys. If he went home and told them he'd only got this far, Trish would give him hell and probably send him back to do it again. It was now or never!

Dan looked in the direction of the house, realising with a shock that the big trees that had once shaded the track to the house were gone. In fact, there was not a tree to be seen in any direction. Without them, there was no softening of the sharp hill line against a harsh blue sky and the drought landscape was unrelenting. The merest hint of where the track had once been rose before him up a gradual slope for about half a mile to the crest of a low hill and then dropped out of sight on the other side into a shallow valley for another half a mile. A mile in this heat. A mile there and a mile back. No trees, no shade, just bare paddocks, dust and heat.

It seemed daunting, but then he thought, when I was a boy, a mile was nothing, I walked for miles and miles as a matter of course, I shouldn't be put off by this. So. Only a mile. There'd be shade somewhere at the house for sure. He could rest, eat and drink there and return to town by lunchtime, as he'd promised his mother.

Not a problem. Just do it.

He took biscuits and snack bars from the cooler and pushed them into a pocket of his cargo shorts, collected the chilled bottle of water, put on his hat and climbed through the barbed wire fence to the left of the gate post. The sun scorched his bare legs and he wished he'd remembered sunscreen. Oh well, it wouldn't be the first time he'd been sunburnt. He'd spent his entire childhood with peeling cheeks, arms and legs.

He strode along the track, dust billowing out behind him in a soft cloud. Within minutes, his socks were wet with sweat and his Nikes felt heavy and uncomfortable. He should have worn sandals. He remembered the avenue of tall shady gums that he'd strolled between as a boy and grieved at the barrenness of bare earth around him.

Only half a mile to the top of the hill. Not far. But it felt far, much farther than he remembered, the distance not seeming any less each time he looked up. Sweat gathered in pools where his sunglasses rested on his cheeks, creeping into the lines around his eyes and stinging. He stopped to wipe away the sweat with his handkerchief and took a swig of water, then pushed the bottle into a pocket.

He could feel the heat getting to him, making him feel irritable and anxious. He remembered this sort of gritty heat as being a natural part of the height of summer, after harvest, when he could spend his school holidays splashing around in the waterhole while Dad napped under a nearby tree. He'd never known it to be like this so early in the season.

A black snake slithered across the track a few yards in front of him. He stopped moving and waited until it had gone, realising as he did so that this was a reaction that belonged to the country boy he had once been. He could hear Mum's voice instructing him, "They don't hurt you if you don't hurt them. Just stand very still, Danny love, and the snake will move on." Suddenly, he was filled with a longing for the way things had been, for the green paddocks of spring, for the cold nights and warm days, for being tucked into bed at night feeling safe and secure with Mum and Dad looking out for him.

A wave of nostalgia overwhelmed him. He remembered the fenced off area near the house that Mum had set up so that he could feed the poddy lambs before school, their little tails shaking with excitement at the sight of him in the early morning light. How soft they felt as he held the bottles to their eager mouths. He remembered Mum standing behind him, arms akimbo, laughing at the top of her voice as a lamb wriggled away from him and milk poured over his legs and feet. It was a shock to remember that laugh. He'd not heard it again for many years after Dad died. In fact, she'd rarely smiled. She hadn't laughed again until after she'd met Terry. He'd brought the laughter back into her life.

Another memory assailed him which made him feel like crying for the want of it. Mum in the harvester at night, the lights illuminating a little patch of golden wheat in front of them, the warm night air caressing their skins as he sat on her lap and steered. He'd feel himself drift off to sleep in her arms and then wake as the sky began to colour, the crows and magpies heralding the day, the smell of sweat and coffee as Mum poured him a wake up drink from the thermos. She'd stop long enough to let him jump to the ground and empty his bladder, then help him back up so that he could steer around the paddocks some more, munching on the Anzac biscuits she'd baked a few nights before. He remembered she never seemed to sleep over the harvesting period. He had a clear image of her weary face smiling at him as they sipped their coffee.

Dan suddenly wondered why Dad hadn't been driving the harvester, then dismissed the thought. Dad would have had other things to do.

Yet another memory of Mum rushed at him. He was home from school with the flu and Mum sat him in the sun on the veranda with a cup of hot lemon and honey. He said he was cold, so she brought a blanket outside, pulled him on to her lap and wrapped the blanket around both of them. They sat in contentment for a long time.

He must have dozed off because the sound of Dad calling out to Mum made him wake suddenly. Mum went off to do something for Dad and left Dan on his own, and he remembered how cold it was without her. He always felt so safe when Mum was around, so special, so important. A little boy who was the centre of his mother's world, with no cares, no worries and no fears. He remembered that feeling and wanted it again so badly that it hurt. It hurt him in the head and in the heart. It hurt so much that he felt it all over his body as a breathless, tingling pain. He wanted to be back in that place in time when the world was wonderful and always would be, a place in time before tragedy, despair and disillusionment.

A willie-willie suddenly sprang up between Dan and the hilltop, a familiar sight from his boyhood, but one which he hadn't seen since he'd left the farm. They'd always fascinated him. One minute, the air seemed still and hot, the next there was a flurry of wind from nowhere, a miniature tornado spinning around its own micro low pressure system, gathering dust and leaves and anything else light enough to be carried into its vortex as it travelled recklessly across the landscape.

Dan paused and waited for it to make its way across the paddock, leaving behind it a swept trail, but it held fast to the track, spinning upon itself and gathering strength. He decided to skirt around it and rejoin the track on its far side, but as he did so, it followed him. He increased his pace, feeling the edge of the willie-willie brushing against his heels, whilst being aware it was growing in size and speed behind him. Looking up, he saw he was only a few yards from the crest of the hill. Without any trees between him and his goal, he knew he'd see the house in another moment. His heart began to race.

With a rush of wind, the willie-willie engulfed him, swirling grit around his face, up his nose, into his eyes and flinging his hat into the air. Removing his sunglasses, he covered his face with his handkerchief and blindly lunged forward, knowing it should move away from him as was its nature, but instead it stayed with him. Grit and debris bit into his skin, his shorts billowed out from his legs and his hair felt as if it was lifting away from his head. He stumbled on and, suddenly, he was moving downhill, the crest behind him.

He felt the willie-willie lose energy as if it was draining away from him. He tried to open his eyes, but they were filled with dust, so he squeezed them shut again and took another couple of steps forward.

He bumped into something smooth and hard and felt the sensation of coolness and moisture. The air was incredibly still and quiet around him. Wiping the grit from his face, he blinked to clear his vision, but immediately closed his eyes again. What he saw was not real.

CHAPTER FOUR

He must have fainted. That was it. He'd concentrate and come around properly now. He opened his eyes again, but it was still there.

Dan was standing beside a big old ghost gum, it's bark like silver in the dappled shade of its branches. A few yards away was another old ghost gum, and then another in a long line of sentinel gums following the curve of the track down to the house. But that wasn't possible. The last owners had cut down every tree on the property and he'd not seen any trees from the other side of the hill. He would have seen these from a great distance. They were huge.

The touch of something soft against his ankles drew his attention downward. Green grass. Lush, emerald green grass. His gaze flowed across rippling green paddocks as far as the eye could see. Then he smelled it, that delicious fragrance of damp air on new grass after rain and saw the rain clouds drawing away towards the hills in the distance.

This was not happening. He was about to close his eyes and attempt to wake up again when his attention was distracted by a laugh coming from the valley below. Coming from where the house should be. He turned to look.

The track flowed downhill away to the right between the elegant gums. Dan knew he was still dreaming, but if he took a few more steps in this dream, would the house appear before him as he remembered it? Would it be just as he wanted it, as it had been before Dad's murder, before horror, fear and confusion had set in? Just a few dream steps, was that all it would take?

Maybe he didn't want to wake up just yet.

So he took a few steps and there it was, appearing before him in stages. First, the orchard of citrus and stone fruit, then the vegetable garden at the edge of sweeping lawns and the tall exotic trees with their leaves glistening after the rain, and finally the rose garden and flagstone paths up to the veranda of the house. The galvanised iron of the shearing and equipment sheds behind the house still glittered with rainwater trickling into the tanks. And surrounding the whole picture was a frame of towering ancient gums, blue-green in the moist post-rain air.

The house was perfect. The red iron roof protected solid sandstone walls ringed by a wide veranda supported by timber posts. Flowering wisteria clambered along the timber lacework on one side, creating a graceful blue and green fringe. The garden served as a verdant frame with splashes of colour from the spring flowers. It looked what it was - prosperous.

Dan stood still, tears threatening to intrude on this dream picture. He thought, I want to remember this when I wake up, then willed himself to end the dream, for he knew he must be lying in the heat and dust of reality with the sun baking his skin and dehydration lying in wait.

Wake now, he commanded himself. Then he heard the laughter again. OK dream, if you insist, I'll linger a little longer.

A laughing boy ran from behind the house, something clutched preciously in his arms. A boy with dark hair and grubby clothes, a boy of about ten or eleven years, with lean limbs and youthful bounce. He called out suddenly, "Mum! There are six now! Come and see!" He leapt onto the veranda, turned and squatted, his hands arranging the bundle he held so that it lay in his lap. It was a puppy, newborn and still wet with birth fluids streaking its black and white fur.

Dan sucked in his breath. He was looking at himself as a boy. What strange tricks this dream was playing on him. How could he see himself like this, from the outside, when all his dreams until now had seen the outside from within himself? He had always been the boy looking out, not someone else looking in.

Now he saw himself holding the puppy and he knew instantly what day this was. Mum had told him that fateful morning that five puppies were expected and already promised to new owners, but that if there were more, then Danny could keep a puppy for himself.

Dan took a few more dream steps until he stood under the big pine tree next to the house-paddock gate. From there, he could see the freckles splashed across young Danny's nose and the sweet innocence of a happy child.

Dan closed his eyes. This memory twisted his heart and shortened his breath. It was too poignant, this last happy day of his life. He didn't want to feel like this. Time to wake up now.

A voice, familiar and dear to him, snapped his eyes open. Mum was standing in the doorway, her long black hair, still damp from the weekly shampoo, hanging over one shoulder as she stroked it smooth with a comb.

This time, Dan could not hold back. The dream tears splashed down his cheeks. This was not the plump, grey haired woman he'd left an hour ago in town. This was the Mum of his boyhood - slender waisted, long tanned legs and arms, skin clear and smooth, and brown eyes soft and warm.

Mum said, "Danny love, what a lucky stroke. Is it a boy or a girl?" She put the comb on the veranda table and squatted next to her son, taking the puppy gently and turning it over. "It's a girl. What are you going to call her?"

Dan mouthed the words silently as young Danny said, "Lucky Six. Lucky for short." The boy looked up. "Is my cake ready yet?"

"It's cooling. Why don't you take Lucky back to her mother while I get things ready?" Danny jumped up and ran back toward the sheds.

Connie stood slowly and turned to go back into the house, but something caught her eye and she turned to look in Dan's direction.

Time to wake up, Dan thought. Time to leave this dream. She can't see me because I'm not real. None of this is real.

But she did see him. She shaded her eyes and looked, then raised her hand high in a greeting, visibly uncertain who it was she was hailing. She came towards him across the green lawn. He felt rooted to the spot.

"Hello!" she called. As she approached, he saw the question in her eyes as she looked behind him for a vehicle, then brought her gaze back to his when she saw none. "Can I help you?"

Wake up! Wake up! He felt panic rise up in him. Then she smiled the welcoming smile of the gracious country woman she was and suddenly he didn't want to wake up, he wanted to stay.

He looked down, aware as he did so that his boyhood memories of his mother at this age were all of looking up. From his adult height, he saw the perfect part of her wet hair, the long black eyelashes curving upward, the short pretty nose and soft full mouth. How old was she here in this dream? If it was his eleventh birthday, then she was twenty-eight. He saw her for the first time as a mature man sees a younger woman and the impact was a shock to him. She was beautiful, simply beautiful.

And yet ... there was a tension in her face, something not quite right. He couldn't pinpoint it at first, then as she raised her face a little, he saw dark bags under her eyes and a pinched quality to the smile. It aged her beyond her twenty-eight years.

"Hello," he said slowly.

Connie stood a few paces from him and looked at him carefully, her lovely head tilted slightly. "Do I know you?" she queried. "You look familiar."

Dan wanted to cry out, "I'm Danny, Mum, look at me, I'm your Danny!" but instead he said, "No, I'm not from around here."

"Oh, OK. I'm Connie Averill." It was a shock to hear his father's surname again. He'd forgotten that Mum had taken her maiden name again after Dad died and insisted

Danny be known as a Campbell too. He'd forgotten that he was once Danny Averill. He'd never understood why she did that.

She waited.

A name was expected. His mind scrambled for one, and the first name to come to him was his firstborn son's, Hamish. So he said, "Hamish," and then added Trish's maiden name, "Walsh".

"Hamish," she repeated, "that was my father's name," and looked over his shoulder again, awaiting an explanation. No one turned up unannounced on foot out here without a good reason.

Once again, he scrambled for something plausible. "My car. It broke down ... out of petrol ... on the road."

She relaxed. This far out of town, it wasn't uncommon for someone to misjudge how much fuel they would need, especially a stranger. "My husband is due back any minute. He'll be able to help you." She glanced at his empty hands. "You didn't have a jerrycan in the boot? No matter, we'll have something in the shed." She turned her head as a noise distracted her. It was young Danny jumping onto the veranda. He turned to watch them.

Connie smiled. "Kettle's on," she said, "fancy a cuppa while you're waiting for my husband?" She led the way to the house. The aroma of freshly baked chocolate cake wafted from the kitchen window.

Dan wanted to look at young Danny, to stare, take it in - himself thirty years ago - but he sensed Danny was staring back at him in that unaffected way children have, so he kept his gaze averted. Then he realised Danny was not looking at his face, but at his shoes. He glanced down. His Nikes were filthy. Perhaps that was it.

"Danny love, this is Mr Walsh. He's run out of petrol up on the road. Go and find Dad, will you?" Danny ran to the end of the veranda, leapt off and headed at full speed toward the sheds. Connie turned to Dan. "You know, it's a long way back to your car and it's almost lunch time. It's Danny's birthday and we're having sandwiches and cake out here in a few minutes. Why don't you stay for lunch?"

Dan smiled. What a beautiful dream. He was assailed with the smells and noises and sensations of his childhood and he no longer wanted to awaken. More than anything, he wanted this moment with his mother and the boy he once was, this last sane, simple day of his life. And he wanted to see his father.

Alec Averill appeared at the end of the veranda in tattered blue overalls, his hands black with grease and smears of grease down one side of his stubbled face. A cigarette hung limply from the corner of his mouth. He paused and looked at Dan. Dan smiled at him, his heart racing, his breath coming in shallow gulps. He wanted to run to his father, to cry out, "Dad! It's me! It's your Danny!" But of course, he didn't. This was a dream and the dream Danny was coming up behind the dream Dad. Dan tried to say hello but the word would not come. Instead it was Dad who spoke first.

"Who the fuck are you?" he said bluntly. Dan was shocked. The voice was nasal, cold, hard. He hadn't remembered it like that, and yet in that second he knew that's what it had been. Dad hadn't even bothered to remove the cigarette. He'd just spat the words out.

Connie stepped forward quickly. "This is Hamish Walsh, Alec. His car ran out of petrol on the road ..."

"Shut up, Con!"

Connie looked down and timidly stepped back.

Dad jumped up onto the veranda, strode to within a couple of feet of Dan and looked up at him challengingly.

Another shock. Dan stood a good eight inches taller than his father. The memory of his father being a tall heroic figure disintegrated. He looked down at Alec Averill and saw him for the first time, man to man.

Dad had been ten years older than Mum, which made him thirty-eight in this dream world, three years younger than the Dan who stood over him now. Dan was six feet tall, broad shouldered, narrow hipped and still something of an athlete, taking an active part in his two son's sporting activities to stay fit and lean. He didn't consider himself a good looking man, but Trish did, so there was a certain confidence about him, a way of walking tall with the assurance of a man well admired.

He looked down at his father and felt jolted. He didn't like what he saw.

Alec had a mean face. Even as he recognised the truth of it, he wondered why it hadn't registered with him as a boy and why his mind felt it important to register it now in this dream. Alec's face was tight, hard, even cruel, his dark eyes narrowed suspiciously, his mouth gripped tightly around the smoking cigarette, his jaw jutting forward in a manner obviously intended to be threatening. A man dangerous to cross. A man already convinced that Dan was up to no good.

"What are you doing out this way? I ain't seen your face around here before."

A rancid odour of stale alcohol, old cigarette smoke and unwashed body rose up around Alec and

Dan saw that his clothes were filthy. The greasy hands had chipped, ragged fingernails, blackened with layers of thick grime. Dark shaggy hair hung about his face and neck in greasy strands. His whole appearance was in complete contrast with Mum's freshly washed and pleasant smelling cleanliness.

Dan was speechless with the horror of the moment.

"You one of those hippy bastards?" Alec was looking at his baggy cargo shorts and Nikes. "Never seen no one looked like you before. Well?" he demanded.

Danny was watching them silently from the end of the veranda.

Dan knew he had to speak, he had to say something. He squeezed the words from his tight throat, unable to take his eyes from Alec's face. "I ran out of petrol ... just up the road ... saw your gates ... sorry to bother you ..."

Please please please let me wake up now. This is too much.

The dream had become a nightmare.

Alec took the cigarette from his mouth and tossed it into the daisy bush next to the veranda. "Yeah, yeah, yeah. You gotta be a city bloke. Only a city bloke would be stupid enough to travel out here without spare fuel on board."

"Yes," Dan stammered, "Yes, I'm from Sydney."

"So what're you doing out here?"

For a second, Dan couldn't think of anything. Then, unexpectedly, he remembered something relevant to this day, something his mother had told him about their neighbours, the Taylors, on the morning of his eleventh birthday.

"I'm a friend of the Taylors. I was travelling in this area and thought I'd call in, but no one was home."

"Well, they wouldn't be, would they? They've had a death in the family and they've all gone to the coast for the funeral. Won't be back for another three days. You didn't know?"

"No. I took a chance on them being home, I know, but I've been on the road for a few days, so I'm a bit out of touch."

"On the road, hey? What are you, some sort of travelling salesman?"

"Yes. I'm a travelling salesman."

"So what're you selling? Hope it's not those weird hippy clothes you're wearing, 'cos you won't make a living selling shit like that around here."

Dan struggled to bring his thoughts back into focus as he cast about for something a travelling salesman might be selling in the country thirty years ago. "Stationery," he said, thinking of the newsagency in town, "I'm selling stationery."

"Stationery?" Alec responded contemptuously. "Sounds like the sort of job a loser would have." He dug deep into a pocket, produced a crumpled pack of cigarettes and quickly lit up. Dan registered that he hadn't been offered one. It was a slight. "Alright. You need petrol. Petrol ain't free, you know. It'll cost you."

Dan wasn't carrying cash, only cards, and cards weren't around in this dream era. He didn't know what to say. Connie saw his confusion and stepped forward again, speaking timidly, carefully.

"Alec, I've asked Mr Walsh to join us for lunch before he goes back. It's Danny's birthday, it would be nice to

have a guest join us, don't you think? Everything's ready
..."

Alec looked at her as if she was stupid. "Jeez, Con, what did you do that for?" He looked back at Dan. "Well, I'm bloody starving. I'm not going nowhere 'til I've had something to eat. Alright. But make it quick, Con. Me and the boy," he looked back at young Danny with a tight smile, "we got things to do, haven't we boy?"

Danny jumped forward. "You haven't seen the puppy, Dad. Come and see the puppy."

"After lunch, boy. After I've got rid of this joker. Alright?" He turned away from Danny and snapped at Connie, "Come on, Con, get on with it. I haven't got all day."

Connie leapt to attention as if whipped and went in to the kitchen. Dad sat in one of the three chairs on the veranda, pointedly not inviting Dan to join him. Danny took another chair and Dan stood awkwardly. He didn't know how to handle this rough, uncouth man. He felt sickened by the whole experience.

Was this what he had come all this way to experience? Did he need to collapse in the heat and dust of his childhood home in order to face some truths his boyhood memory had refused to confront?

Why can't I wake up, he cried silently, why can't I stop this?

Connie appeared with a fourth chair from the kitchen and placed it next to Danny. "Have a seat, Mr Walsh, please. I'll have lunch ready in a jiffy."

"Can I help?" Dan asked, as he normally would in such a situation.

Alec sneered and looked up at Dan. "Help? That's woman's work. What are you, some sort of poofter? Do I have to be worrying about my boy being around you?" Dan was stunned. "Well? Are you or aren't you?"

"Am I what?" Dan asked, confused.

"A bloody poofter? What, are you deaf as well?"

"Alec, please don't ..." Connie pleaded, looking embarrassed and distraught. Danny seemed completely unaware of the tension. "It's Danny's birthday, couldn't we make it nice ..."

"Alright, alright!"

"Is my cake ready?" Danny asked.

Relieved to be distracted, Connie said with mock cheerfulness, "Sure is, Danny. I'll bring it out with the sandwiches." She went into the kitchen and came back quickly with a tray laden with sandwiches, teapot, cutlery, crockery and an iced chocolate cake covered in chocolate sprinkles and topped with eleven candles. A small parcel wrapped in bright paper was placed in the centre of the table. She spent a moment arranging everything and then handed the parcel to Danny.

"Happy birthday, Danny love."

Danny ripped the paper off, Connie gathering it up as he scattered it around. His face lit up with pleasure. "A camera! Thanks, Mum."

Connie leaned across to him. "It's an Instamatic. You don't have to roll the film on, you just put this cartridge in," she opened the back of the camera and clicked the cartridge into place, "like this. It takes twenty four pictures and you can tell how many are left by this number on the back. And it's got a built-in flash for taking pictures inside. I've got a spare cartridge in the kitchen. You can take some pictures of Lucky Six."

"Yeah? This is great, Mum." He turned to his father expectantly. "Can I have it now, Dad?"

Alec blew smoke towards his son with careless indifference. "Soon," he said.

Danny looked disappointed, then resigned, and turned his attention to the camera.

Connie poured Alec a cup of tea, adding milk and sugar. "How do you have your tea, Mr Walsh?"

"Black, no sugar," he responded automatically.

"Oh, same as me," Connie smiled warmly.

Alec looked up. Something in his wife's voice bothered him. "So?" he snapped. "Doesn't make you sweethearts or nothing, does it?"

"I didn't mean anything, Alec." Connie suddenly looked terrified.

Dan didn't understand at first what was happening, but Dad's next words made it clear. He took the cigarette from his mouth and gave Dan and Connie a suspicious look. "You two ain't on together, are you? Is that why you turned up out of the blue? Is it?" The suspicion in his face grew with every word. "Did you come here to see her?" He stabbed the air with his cigarette. "You know I'll bloody kill the pair of you if you're on together!"

"No, Alec, no ..."

Dan rose. The nightmare was out of control and he had to leave it. He had to leave it now. "That's nonsense. I ran out of petrol and came here looking for help. Nothing more. Nothing less. And if my presence disturbs you, then I'll leave." He turned to go.

Connie was clutching her hands to her chest, watching Alec with a look of dread on her stricken face. Danny appeared to be intensely interested in his new toy, removing himself from the ugly reality around him.

"Without petrol?" Alec sneered. "What you gunna do, walk back to town?"

Dan heard Connie gulp with repressed tears. "Alec, please don't, please don't spoil this for Danny. I've never seen Mr Walsh before, I promise. Please, let's just eat and light the candles."

Alec gave her a contemptuous look. "Yeah, yeah, alright. Christ, who'd have you anyway, hey? You ain't exactly the catch of the district. And don't turn on the waterworks, it just makes you look worse than you already do." He dragged deeply on his cigarette, then turned towards the food as if nothing had happened.

Connie said quickly, apologetically, "Please, sit down, Mr Walsh, we'll light the candles in a moment."

Dan sat rigidly, afraid to look at her face in case Alec started up again.

Connie turned to Danny with forced cheerfulness and said, "OK, Danny love? We'll get on with it, shall we?" She took Alec's box of matches and lit the candles.

Alec suddenly slapped his thigh and began singing raucously, "Happy Birthday to you!" Connie joined in softly and Dan felt compelled to join in too. He looked at Danny's delighted face and his heart twisted. Had he really been this naive, this unaware?

The song finished and Danny looked at Alec with anticipation. "Can I have it now, Dad? Please, please, please?"

"Yeah, why not." Alec rose, went in to the house . He returned with a small rifle and a box of bullets in one hand, and an open bottle of beer in the other. He passed the gun to Danny without ceremony. Danny grabbed it and looked it over with excitement.

Dan finished his cup of tea and slice of cake because it seemed like he should, wondering at the realness of their taste and texture. This was a powerful dream. He remembered clearly the thrill of that moment when he got the rifle for his birthday, but he had no recollection of the rest of this birthday lunch on the veranda. What would happen next? He felt fear. Maybe he didn't want to know. His heart was racing.

Alec swigged from the beer bottle, smacking his lips loudly with pleasure. Dan saw Connie flinch at the noise. The tension between his parents was palpable.

Dan hated this. He wanted to snap his fingers and make it end. If he couldn't will himself to wake up, then perhaps he could control the direction of the dream. He stood up and said, "I should be going." He remembered the need for petrol and the money issue. "I don't have any cash with me, but ..." he looked down at his wrist, "I do have this watch which is worth much more than a can of petrol. Would you accept this as payment?" He removed it and passed it to Alec.

"Looks like a kid's toy to me," Alec said, "I ain't never seen a watch like this before. Don't look like a watch at all. What're trying to pull here, hey?"

"It's a digital watch."

"Digital? Never heard of it. It don't even have a watchface." He tried to pass it back, but Dan held it before him.

"The time shows in hours, minutes and seconds here on this display. The date is here. The button here lights up the display for reading it at night. It's waterproof, you access a menu here to show you international times, it can be a calculator ..."

"Jeez, does it shag the missus, too?" Alec sniggered. "What's it worth?"

"It's worth a week's salary."

Alec's hand closed around the watch. "Alright. Deal. Wait here. I'll get a jerrycan and throw it in the back of the ute."

"No, you don't need to do that. I'll walk back to the car. I can leave the empty can by the gate. No need for you to go to any more trouble."

Alec rose. "Fine by me. I'll get the fuel. Come on boy, you can help me." With a warning sideways glance at Connie, he strode toward the sheds, Danny running behind him.

Connie watched them go, then turned to Dan. "I'm sorry, Mr Walsh. He's not usually ..." She stopped. To claim that her husband was not usually inhospitable would be too obviously a lie. She opened her mouth to try again, but Dan interrupted.

"It's alright, really it is." But it wasn't alright. Connie's face was flushed with embarrassment and humiliation. He wanted desperately to reach out to her, to cry out, "I didn't know, Mum! I didn't remember how he was." And yet, even as he thought it, he did remember. He remembered finding his mother crying alone in the kitchen after Dad had yelled at her. He remembered that Dad yelled at her a lot. He remembered turning his nose up at the smell of Dad. And he remembered Dad drinking himself into a stupor, slumped in the chair out here on the veranda or in the chair pulled close to the wood stove in the kitchen.

Why hadn't he remembered all this before? Perhaps it was the trauma of what happened later that had made him shut out the bad memories. Or maybe it was simply that a boy needed to remember only the good things about his father.

His mother had always encouraged the good memories. Spotlighting at night for kangaroos, rabbits and foxes, fishing and swimming in the waterhole, yabbying in the nearby creek. She'd never spoken of the nasty side of Dad, of the drinking, the yelling, the laziness...

The laziness. Memories came rushing at him unchecked. Mum seeding after the rains while Dad slept off the alcohol, Mum up on a ladder fixing the leaking roof while Dad drank and smoked on the veranda, Mum harvesting all through the night to get the crop in, Mum on the motorbike rounding up sheep for shearing, Mum working with the dogs to herd sheep onto the truck to take to market.

And what was Dad doing when he wasn't drinking or sleeping? Fishing. Shooting. Doing wheelies in the ute. Just mucking about with his son.

That's why he remembered his childhood as full of fun. Dad had included his son in his lazy pursuits, or maybe he had used young Danny as the excuse, like two kids with nothing better to do, while Mum carried the burden of running the farm and keeping them all fed and housed.

No wonder she looked so lean and tanned. She worked as hard as any man. But she also looked haggard, old beyond her years, at the end of her tether. She might be strong and stoic, but she was also worn out.

He hadn't seen that as a boy.

All these revelations came to Dan within the space of a couple of seconds. He felt sick. So was this what he needed to face about his past? It was cruel. But it didn't mean Dad had deserved to die at the hands of a mad stranger.

Then it occurred to Dan that maybe this dream was meant to keep him trapped until he saw the stranger come. If he stayed close by, would he see who it was, remember details about him that he could awaken with later on and take back to the police? He felt dizzy with it all.

Danny came running back from the shed and helped himself to more cake. He appeared disinterested in the visitor on the veranda. "Can I bring Lucky back here now, Mum?"

"Sit down while you eat, Danny love. No, she's too little yet. She needs to stay close to her mother and the other puppies for the next few weeks. When she's weaned, we'll put a blanket on the veranda for her and keep her separate from the working dogs. She can be your dog then." Danny nodded and shoved cake into his mouth. Connie continued, "Where's the camera? And the rifle? You shouldn't leave those things lying around in the shed."

"I'm still taking pictures of the puppies, Mum. Is that alright? And I want to try out the rifle. Dad said I could shoot some bottles off the fence later. I promise I'll bring them back when I've finished."

"That's alright. Did you leave the rifle with the safety on? You know the rules."

"Sure, Mum, I always do that. Can I have the rest of the cake? I'm real hungry."

"Of course, love, it's your birthday, help yourself." Connie seemed to have recovered her composure a little. She turned to Dan. "Your accent reminds me of my mother. She was English. Are you English, Mr Walsh?"

"I was born in Australia," he replied without thinking, his mind still whirling.

"Oh."

Dan felt her uncertainty about what to say next and turned to look at her. It was only then, as she raised her hand to brush her hair away from her face, that he noticed the darkened skin just below her sleeve and again on her neck. It was bruising. Recent bruising. She saw him looking and quickly dropped her arm, turning her face away.

Alec appeared with the jerrycan of fuel. He dropped it at Dan's feet and went inside without a word. Dan had been dismissed.

There was nothing for it but to leave. Dan picked up the jerrycan and turned to Connie. "Thanks for the ..." he began with automatic politeness, but Alec's voice cut through his words.

"Con! Get in here!" Connie flinched as if she'd been slapped, turned without hesitation and went into the house.

Dan was left alone with Danny. He looked down at him, looked directly into his face for the first time, and smiled. "Happy birthday, young man," he said gently.

Danny responded with an effortless grin. "Thanks." He was picking at the last of the cake.

Dan said persuasively, "Go on, finish it off." Danny's grin widened and he scooped up the cake in pieces. The grin quickly became covered in chocolate crumbs.

Dan's heart was breaking. If only he could change things, if only this wasn't a dream. If only this boy before him, this boy who was him, could stay like this, could progress through the rest of his life with his mother and father on the farm.

As he thought it, Dan realised that the boy before him was on the brink of awareness. It would have only been a matter of time, a few months perhaps, a year at the most, before he understood his father's true nature and what it was doing to his mother. He would have grown to hate his father and pity his mother. Or worse – he might have grown to be just like his father with contempt for his mother.

Unbidden, two scenarios played simultaneously across his mind.

Danny growing into Dan after Dad's death, grieving but healing with his mother's devoted care, the wrench of leaving the farm and the move to England, the uncertain times before he made friends at his new school, meeting Terry for the first time and watching his mother blossom from that moment on, his years at university in London, meeting Trish at the graduation party, his marriage, his children, his career in computers and then later taking over the pub. His life, his good, good life.

Or

Danny growing into Dan with Dad alive, running from Dad when he became violent, then one day stepping in to stop Dad from beating Mum, taking the beatings in her place, leaving school early to work on the farm when he saw Mum becoming ill from the strain, fighting with his father, living the violence he learned, drinking young to deal with his own disillusionment and anger, directing his angst towards everyone he dealt with, unable to leave because he couldn't desert Mum, unable to get out with her for fear of Dad following them, his manhood corrupted by a violent adolescence he couldn't escape.

Young Danny was looking up at him curiously. "You alright, mister?" he asked. "You look kinda funny."

Dan said, "Yes, I'm fine," but his mind screamed, I've got to get out of here! He turned and walked away. He wanted to run but the jerrycan weighed him down, so he walked as fast as he could. In a moment, he'd reached the house-paddock gate. As he opened it, he heard a crash followed by a scream behind him. Connie's scream. Turning quickly, he saw Danny standing on the veranda looking into the house. Then Danny turned and looked uncertainly towards Dan.

Dan's universe shifted sideways, for as Danny turned towards him, he became Danny standing on the veranda looking up towards the gate, looking at the stranger. The memory of it was as sharp as the present reality of being Dan looking back at the boy, but it was more than just memory. He was in both places at the same time. He was himself in two different times. He, Dan with the memories of being Danny, knew Dad would yell to go play with the puppies. He, Danny would obey because he didn't want to confront what was happening inside the house.

With shattering realisation, in that instant Dan saw that this twisted nightmare without end had dumped him into the stranger's body. He was the stranger standing under the pine tree with the jerrycan in his hand.

He was the stranger who had killed his father.

The jerrycan slipped from his grasp. His vision blurred and he couldn't breathe. Then he heard Dad yell out as he knew he would, "Get out of here, boy! Go play with the dogs! Go on! Get!" Dan heard it in two places, loud from the veranda and distant from the gate.

He, Danny on the veranda, jumped and ran from the sound of his mother whimpering in the kitchen, ran from what he didn't want to know.

But he, Dan at the gate, wanted to know. Could he go to his mother's aid now? Could he stop his father from beating her? Could he change things?

He must.

But he couldn't move, he had no control over his body. A shuddering weakness swept through him. Then he saw Danny running toward the sheds, saw him as separately as the two of them were physically separate and knew he was no longer both of them. The weakness passed and he breathed again.

There was silence. No more noise came from within the house. None of the other players in this nightmare were to be seen. There was a moment of tranquillity. He tried to pull his fragmented thoughts together.

If this nightmare was putting him into the body of the stranger, it was for a reason. The improbability of it was too hard to comprehend, but his logical mind pursued the path that, if he was being given the opportunity to be the stranger, then he was being given the opportunity to discover what had happened thirty years ago on his eleventh birthday. He reached deep down into his memories for details.

He remembered his mother saying that the stranger had left the farm with the jerrycan after lunch and didn't return until the evening, when the murder took place. In that case, he shouldn't go back inside. But he couldn't stand here and listen to Mum being beaten.

The kitchen door opened and Alec appeared on the veranda. Dan stepped back into the shadow of the tree behind him, but the movement caught Alec's attention. "Thought you'd bloody gone," he called out angrily, then quickly went back into the house. Before Dan could think what to do next, Alec reappeared with a rifle in his hands. He raised it without hesitation and fired. The bullet kicked up the dirt at Dan's feet, making him jump back. This was a dream, so a bullet couldn't really hurt him, but he was as afraid as if he might feel the real thing slice through his body at any moment.

Alec leapt from the veranda and raised the rifle again. "Take your petrol and get out of here, you loony bastard," he screamed. "Don't let me see your face around here again or the next shot'll hit more than the dirt!"

The sight of his father's crazed face galvanised Dan into action. He picked up the jerrycan, turned and sprinted through the gate and up the track. He kept going until he reached the rise, then looked back. Alec was standing in the gateway with the rifle held loosely under one arm, watching him. Dan quickly turned away and kept going.

He was at the crest of the hill. Shouldn't the nightmare end here and return him to his inertia in the heat and dust? But he wasn't to be released from this torment yet. Instead, the tree shaded track stretched before him to the front gate. Fear of the gun-toting man behind him kept his feet moving forward.

When he reached the gate, he looked back again. Alec was nowhere to be seen. He dropped the jerry can and leaned against the stone pillar, his heart pounding and sweat pouring from his body. The dirt road that ran alongside the property was empty, his vehicle nowhere in sight.

He couldn't just keep going. There was nowhere to go.

CHAPTER FIVE

What to do now?

Dan sat down on a rock and discovered that he was trembling. He needed to steady himself and reached into his pocket for the snack bars, biscuits and water bottle. He ate and drank, then dropped the wrappings and the water bottle next to the jerrycan. Would the real things still be in his pocket when he woke with real hunger and thirst? For now, his dream thirst was sated by the dream water and the trembling abated.

Dan thought, OK. If this dream is giving me the opportunity to be the stranger, and the stranger didn't go back to the house until later that evening, then I have the afternoon to fill. I want to see if Mum is alright. I want to see what he did to her. I know Danny played with the puppies, for that is what I remember most about that day. I played with the puppies for most of the afternoon and kept away from the house. So what was Dad doing? If I go back now, will I see him? Will this dream create something for me to see?

Going back to the house seemed like the only thing to do, but he had to return unseen. He thought some more about that. If young Danny was in the shed with the dogs, then he needed to approach the house from the other side to avoid alerting the dogs. He stood up and looked down the fence line toward the west. He remembered that this paddock went for about half a mile, then another fence ran through scrub back to the house paddock. He'd be unseen if he approached from that direction.

He walked quickly along the fence line. No cars went past and he remembered that this road was only frequented by those who lived along it, and they were few and far between. When he reached the patch of scrub, he turned towards the house. The fence here followed the natural curve of a creek bed flanked by low scrub, sweeping around to meet the house-paddock fence behind the orchard.

It took him almost an hour to reach the orchard. He took up a position behind the orange tree and watched the house, but it was difficult to see anything from there.

Mum kept her gardening tools in a small galvanised iron shed not far from this side of the house. The roof of this shed was flat, but sloped slightly away from the house. Dan moved quickly between the fruit trees. A ladder lay on the ground next to the shed. He picked it up and rested it against the side of shed, taking only a couple of seconds to climb it and find a place on the shed roof that felt solid enough to take his weight. He stretched out flat on his belly and peered over the edge of the roof. From here, he could see into three rooms on this side of the house.

The front side window was large with the kitchen sink and table clearly visible through it. The middle window was the dining room, never used and with curtains always drawn. The back window was his boyhood bedroom with the narrow iron bedstead and clutter of boy's things on the dressing table.

It was the open kitchen window that drew his attention. Alec sat on one of the kitchen chairs, his feet thrown up casually on the table, his arms crossed and his head lolling to one side. He appeared to be dozing.

Connie sat hunched across from him, shaking and breathing heavily, her head down, silent tears dripping from her nose and chin. A dribble of blood from a cut on her cheek mingled with the tears. Red swelling from the beating disfigured the side of her face.

The rifle lay on the table between them. Scattered around the rifle were several empty beer bottles and an overflowing ashtray. A space had been cleared in front of Connie and something smeared across the table surface. Dan gave himself a moment for his eyes to adjust to the low light in the kitchen and focused on the smear.

The word SLUT had been written on the table top. Written in red. Written in blood.

Alec had dipped a finger into the bleeding wound on his wife's battered face and scrawled the obscenity before her.

Dan felt sick. His head began to throb and he moved a little to make himself more comfortable, his foot knocking the gutter on the shed roof as he did so. The sound made Alec jump. He opened his eyes, leaned forward to grab the rifle and peered suspiciously into Connie's face. She didn't move.

Alec looked around the kitchen. He hadn't imagined the noise. He rose and went to the window, calling out, "That you, boy?" When no answer came, he sat down again, dropped the rifle nonchalantly on the table, pulled the packet of cigarettes from his pocket and lit up.

Dan froze, too afraid to move a muscle, too afraid to breathe. Every instinct in him wanted to go to his mother's aid, but the rifle on the table immobilised him. It was the same rifle that had killed his father on that terrible day. Why was this nightmare showing him this scene? He tried to find a reason, tried to understand what it should be telling him, but he only felt bewildered.

Then Alec spoke. "Had enough of this shit," he said through a cloud of smoke. "You don't come across, you can get out. You and the boy."

Connie slowly raised her swollen face to look at her husband with empty, defeated eyes. "You get what you want, don't you?" she whispered.

"Yeah, but you don't give it willingly."

"Would you know the difference?"

"The others give it willingly. I know the bloody difference."

"You pay the others to give it willingly, but would they without the money?"

"Sometimes I pay. Sometimes I don't need to. But I'm sick of going into town for what I could be getting here for nothing. If you don't give it to me nicely like the girls in town, then you can get out and I'll bring someone out here who'll fuck when I want it."

"That's all I mean to you then, is it, Alec? The nearest vacant vagina?"

Alec sneered. "That's all any bloody sheila is worth. You're all the same as far as I'm concerned. So here's the deal. You can stay. You can leave. Up to you. But if you stay, you gotta behave. If you leave, everything here is mine and I get myself a bit of arse that's willing."

"You can't do that. The farm is mine. Nothing here is in your name. If I leave, I'll sell up and you'll have nothing."

Alec squinted through the smoke. "Been thinking about that. You tried to leave a couple of times before. Remember what I did to you when I found you?"

"I remember. You beat me and raped me. Like you always do. Like you've been doing since I was seventeen. Only last time you said you'd hurt Danny if I ever tried to leave again. So I've stayed."

"Yeah. Fat lot of good it's done me, though. You ain't changed, you're still a cold bitch like you always was."

"I'm not cold, Alec, but you raped me the first night we met. Not exactly a good start to a relationship."

Alec sniggered. "Good a start as any, if you ask me. Only way I was gunna get a bit from a frigid bitch like you."

"It was deliberate, wasn't it, Alec? To get me pregnant. If that time hadn't worked, would you have come for me again?"

"That was the plan. You was an easy mark, Con. But it did work, didn't it?

"Yes," she whispered through bloodied lips. "You got me pregnant and then you convinced my parents you should marry me, convinced them that you loved me and that you'd take care of me and the baby. Only Dad wasn't really convinced, was he? He never liked you, but Mum said it was the best thing for the baby. I was only seventeen. You beat me on our wedding night and you've been beating me and raping me ever since. You called me a cold bitch. I don't know who I am without you, Alec, but I know that in my heart I'm not cold."

63

"You don't know who you are without me? I know who you are. You're nothing!" He slammed his fist down of the table, but Connie didn't flinch. She was beyond physical response. "You were nothing when I met you and you'll always be nothing. You should be glad someone wanted to fuck you when you was seventeen 'cos no other bloke wanted you. If I hadn't taken you out behind the town hall at the dance that night, you'd be an ugly old maid. You wouldn't have the boy. You'd be out here on your own. You'd have nothing." He sucked on his cigarette, exhaled noisily, and flicked ash towards her, annoyed by her composure. "You wanna get out, don't you?"

"Yes."

"Well, I figured out a way. Here's what you gotta do. You gotta sign the place over to me. Lock, stock and barrel. When you done that, you can go. And take the boy with you. He's a bloody nuisance anyway."

Connie looked at him steadily. "I can't do that, Alec."

"Course you can."

"No, I can't. When Dad died, the will stated that the property was to be left to me and that in the event of my death, it would pass to Danny. But there was something else written into the will that prevented it from ever being signed over to you." She paused. "It's almost like he knew it would come to this."

Alec smiled maliciously. "Funny 'bout that."

"What do you mean?"

"Remember how he died?"

"He had a heart attack while he was seeding the north paddock a few weeks after Danny was born."

"Maybe."

A spark in Connie's eyes was the only indication that she'd become more alert. The rest of her remained perfectly still.

"What do you mean?"

"We had a little chat that day, me and your old man."

"A chat?"

"Yeah. He wanted me to leave. Said he'd seen the bruises on you and he was afraid I'd turn on the boy next. Told me I was no good and he'd made a big mistake letting us get married. Said you'd have been better off having the kid without me." Alec took a swig from the beer bottle. He was enjoying this. "I told him his daughter was a fucking whore and the kid wasn't mine anyway. Told him you'd had half the district inside your pants before I came on the scene."

Connie tensed as a look of horror crossed her face. "You know Danny's your son. I was a virgin that night and there has never been anyone else."

"I know that and you know that, but he didn't. He didn't believe me, but it made him real angry. Took a swipe at me but missed by a mile. Then I told him the only reason I'd claimed the brat was mine was so I could get my hands on this place. Once he was dead, the farm would be mine. But he said he'd taken care of that. Said he'd had a new will written up after your mother died. Said he'd made sure I couldn't ever get my hands on it. Everything went to you and then the bloody boy. So I said what if the boy's dead?"

Connie brought one hand up to rest on the table. Alec jerked forward and grabbed the rifle. He lay it across his knees and smirked at her again. "Yeah, that shook him up. Said he'd made sure that if you were both dead that

65

the property would be sold up and I sure as hell couldn't afford to buy it. Said it was a condition of inheritance you'd have to agree to before you got the place. Said he'd had it written in the terms of the will which set it in concrete, there was nothing I could do about it. He was frothing at the mouth by then. Tried to provoke me into a fight, but I didn't want no marks on him."

"No marks? Alec ... what did you do out there?"

"Nothing much. In fact, it was too bloody easy. He was so worked up, it was easy to push him off his feet, push him so he lay face down in the damp soil. Then all I had to do was hold him there." He let the implication of his words sink in.

Connie's eyes widened as the truth hit her. "You killed him? But the coroner said he'd had a heart attack."

"He did, didn't he, with his face buried in the dirt and his arms and legs jerking all over the place. Then all I had to do was leave him there, come back to the house, tell you I hadn't seen him and let you find him out there next to the tractor."

Her breath coming in short shocked gasps, Connie stood suddenly, knocking the chair over behind her.

"Sit down! You ain't going nowhere." Alec raised the rifle and aimed it at her heart.

"You wouldn't, Alec, you wouldn't really, not with Danny outside."

Alec laughed, a sinister sound that cut through the room. He lowered the rifle. "Nah, not yet. Not until I got what I want. And what I want is this place. I figured out a way to get it, see? That smart arse will doesn't say anything about who you can sell this place to, does it? Just says I can't get my hands on it if you're both dead and you can't sign it over to me while you're alive. Signing it over ain't selling it, though, is it? Signing over means no money changing hands, but someone giving you some money for the place makes it a sale. You can sell the place any time you want to anyone you want. So I wanna buy it. I wanna buy it tomorrow. We go into town and see that lawyer, we tell him you're selling out to me, that we got an agreement about the price and we don't have to give him a reason 'cos it's nothing to do with nobody but us. I reckon a couple of thousand will do it, we got that much in the bank. That'll be enough to make it legal. Then when it's all signed and sealed and I got the papers in my hand, you and the brat can go. That's the price for your freedom. You want out. I want this place."

Connie sat stiffly with wide, frightened eyes. "Would you really let us go? Would you give me a divorce?"

The sinister smirk returned. "A divorce? Now that's another matter entirely. Maybe I'll give you a divorce. Maybe not. Once this place is mine, I can do what I like, can't I?" he taunted. "And while you're my wife, I can do what I like with you, too? Maybe I'll let you go, maybe I'll keep you here to … play with. Maybe I'll just get rid of the boy."

"What are you saying?"

"Well, if I get rid of the boy, then I can do what I like with you, can't I? Pisses me off, the way you're always mollycoddling him, sending him off all the time so's he don't hear you snivelling and whining."

"You can't do that."

"I can do whatever the fuck I want! He's a pest. I can say he's wild, we can't do nothing with him. One of them churchy people would take him in."

"No, Alec, no …"

Alec slammed the table again. "I told you! I can do whatever the fuck I like and you can't do nothing about it. Tomorrow, I get what I want, once and for all, and you'll bloody do what you're told after that. What happens to you is up to me and nobody but me. Got it?" He leaned back with an arrogance that knew no bounds.

Connie turned and looked out of the kitchen window. On the shed roof, Dan tried to duck down, but he was already lying flat against the roof. He needn't have worried. Connie's eyes were turned inward, seeing something visible only to herself. "Tomorrow," she said quietly.

"Yeah. Tomorrow." Alec swigged until the bottle was empty and yawned. "I'm gunna have a nap," he said calmly, believing that everything was settled. "Keep the boy out of my way. I don't wanna be disturbed." He rose unsteadily, leaned the rifle against the side of the fridge and headed towards the bedroom.

CHAPTER SIX

Connie watched him go, then looked down at the word written on the table in her own blood. She passed her hand over it slowly, then again, then rubbed at it in a frenzy until her hand was red and the table was clean. She held her hand in front of her and stared at it, stared at it for a long time. Then her face crumpled and a loud despairing sob heralded a weeping session that Dan found unbearable to watch.

He must go to her. It didn't matter that none of this was real, that it was nothing more than a bad dream. He felt her anguish as deeply as if everything he had witnessed had really happened. He began to move towards the ladder, but sudden footsteps on the veranda drew his attention back to the kitchen.

Danny burst into the kitchen, the camera in one hand and the birthday rifle in the other. Connie stood quickly and bent over the kitchen sink to wash her hands, her battered face turned away from her son. As Dan saw this, he remembered many such times in the kitchen when his mother had seemed busy at the sink.

"Look, Mum. I didn't use all the pictures. I kept some for later," Danny declared, holding the camera out to her. "I got four pictures left."

"You did well. Put it on the fridge, love," Connie replied with effort, her black hair veiling her face.

69

Danny leapt to obey. "I'm going to practise shooting some bottles now."

"No, Danny, your father's having a sleep. You'll have to find something quieter to do."

"But, Mum …"

"Do as I ask. You know he gets cranky if he's disturbed. Perhaps after he wakes up, alright?"

"But, Mum …"

"No arguments, Danny love. Leave the rifle here and go back with the puppies for now. Lucky Six needs to spend lots of time with you. Stay with the puppies for the rest of the afternoon. Alright?"

Danny sulked as he put his rifle next to his father's larger weapon. "Alright. But Dad said …"

Connie raised a hand to stop him. Danny knew what that meant. There was no point in pursuing this any further. Instead, he said, "I'm hungry."

Without lifting her head, Connie reached into the cupboard above her and pulled out a packet of biscuits. "Take these. And there's a lemonade in the fridge. Take the bottle. That should tide you over until tea time. Alright?"

"Alright." Danny took the biscuits and lemonade and ran outside. Dan knew that Danny wouldn't be back until Dad called him for tea later that afternoon.

Connie sighed heavily and sagged onto a chair. She leaned forward to rest her head gently on folded arms, her face turned away from the window. Dan waited. She stayed very still and very quiet for a long time. He thought she might be sleeping, but then she lifted her head slowly and turned to look at the two rifles by the fridge. She looked at them for several minutes, then rose slowly, picked up Alec's rifle and slid the safety bolt into place. He was always leaving the rifle lying around with the safety off and she was particular about gun safety. She'd been born on a farm with firearms and had learned good habits from her father, but Alec had always been careless about such things.

As she replaced the rifle, something crossed her face. A thought. It clearly disturbed her for she shook her head and looked away. Then she brought her gaze back to the rifle. Again, she was very still for a very long time. Then she looked up at the cupboard she'd taken the biscuits from earlier, reached into it and took out a pill bottle.

Dan remembered that Mum had taken sleeping tablets when he was a boy. She'd kept them in that cupboard. She'd have a couple with her cup of tea after they'd eaten the evening meal. Now, she removed the cap and tipped the small, white tablets into the palm of her hand. There were plenty of them.

Suddenly, she scooped them back into the bottle, pushed them away from her and began to weep. Deep, heaving sobs that shuddered through her body. Dan heard her wheeze through the sobs, "Tomorrow, tomorrow, tomorrow." She wept and wept, collapsing back onto the chair. Finally, the weeping exhausted her into stillness and she sat staring out the window with swollen unseeing eyes.

Dan could see that she was working through something. She cried a little more, then stopped and thought again. She did this on and off throughout the afternoon. Dan became stiff and achy on the shed roof and wondered how long he'd been lying in the heat and dust in the real world. He was grateful for the illusion of shade from a nearby tree as he watched his mother's torment. The moment to go to her had long since passed. He was merely a spectator in this dreamworld, but the scene before him was breaking his heart nevertheless.

After another long period of stillness, Connie rose slowly and picked up Alec's rifle. She loaded it, took the safety catch off and replaced it, then went through the same process with Danny's rifle. She stared at them, one hand over her mouth and the other held across her chest. When she finally turned away, it was with a look of disconnected resignation.

Connie began to move around the kitchen as if she was sleepwalking, picking things up and putting them away without appearing to see them. Cleaning the table of blood, beer and cigarettes, she began to cook as she always did at this time of day, peeling carrots and potatoes at the sink, shelling peas, taking sausages from the fridge, stoking up the wood stove and getting saucepans and frypan, all done in a dreamlike state. A bunch of rhubarb she'd picked earlier that day went into a saucepan with sugar, and she added eggs to another saucepan of milk to make a custard.

As she turned towards the window, Dan saw that her eyes was glazed and dull, like a dead person's. The sight chilled Dan's soul. He was afraid for her.

The call of nature intruded on the nightmare. Dan needed to empty his bladder. Even though none of this was real, the urge felt strong enough to dictate his next move and could no longer be ignored. He waited until Connie was in the pantry before he slid across the roof and down the ladder. Moving quickly, he went to the edge of the orchard and did what he needed to do. The orchard was casting long shadows in the late afternoon light.

Silently taking up his position on the shed roof again, he saw Connie at the kitchen sink with a rolling pin in her hands. The bottle of sleeping pills lay on the chopping board in front of her. She removed the cap and poured them carefully onto the board. Then she crushed them slowly, carefully under the rolling pin until they were a fine white powder.

The next thing she did took Dan by surprise. She carried the chopping board to the stove and tipped the powder into the custard, scraping every last grain off with a knife.

There were enough pills in that custard to kill a person. To kill several people.

A shock of adrenalin went through him. Was she planning to kill Alec? That couldn't be because he suddenly remembered that Dad hated custard, especially rhubarb and custard. He remembered Dad calling it old folk slops. He wouldn't eat the stuff, no matter what.

Then who? Herself?

Then he remembered that rhubarb and custard had been one of his favourite childhood desserts.

No. That wasn't possible. She wasn't planning to poison her own son.

Was she?

A door slammed somewhere in the house. Alec appeared, wiping a sleep fuzzed face with his greasy hand. "Tea ready?" he demanded.

"Almost," Connie responded woodenly.

"Good. I'm bloody starving. Where's the boy?"

"He's in the shed with the puppies."

"Those bloody puppies. I'd drown the lot of them if they weren't worth a few quid. I'll get him, but make sure tea's on the table when we get back." He went outside and returned a few minutes later with Danny.

"Go and wash up, love," she said gently, her head turned away again. Danny went into the bathroom.

Alec sat at the table and waited to be served. Connie moved around the kitchen like an automaton, setting the table, straining the vegetables, serving the food onto plates. The three of them sat in silence, although Danny was visibly restless, swinging his legs under the table and looking out through the screen door. But not a word was said. Alec didn't like chatter at meal times.

Alec and Danny wolfed their food down, but Connie only picked at hers without eating anything. She rose to remove the plates and put three dessert bowls on the kitchen sink.

Danny said, "Can I go see Lucky again before I go to bed, Mum?"

Alec snapped irritably, "Sleep with them if you like. Just shut up and finish your tea."

"You can visit her one more time as soon as you've finished dessert, love, but be quick," Connie interceded. She turned back to the bowls on the sink.

Dan watched with horror as she ladled custard and rhubarb into one of the bowls and gave it to Danny, who gulped down the first few mouthfuls. Tinned peaches went into the bowls for Alec and herself. "Where's the cream?" Alec demanded.

Connie went to the fridge. As she did so, Danny jumped up behind her, went to the sink, tipped the remaining custard out and quickly washed it away as he made a show of cleaning his plate. "I've finished, Mum, can I go now?"

She turned towards him, gave him a long look, and asked, "Did you finish all of it, Danny love?"

"Sure, Mum. Can I go now?"

"Yes, but only for a few minutes. It's been a big day, you need an early night."

"Just bloody go," Alec snapped again. "Can't a man get any bloody peace while he's eating?"

Danny ran outside.

Connie sat at the table with the peaches and cream untouched before her. Even from the shed roof, Dan could see her hands shaking. Her face had swelled and coloured since the beating. He wondered that Danny hadn't noticed, whereas Alec seemed smugly satisfied by his wife's appearance.

Alec finished his meal and took a bottle of beer and his smokes out onto the veranda. Connie began clearing up as if nothing out of the ordinary was happening. As she wiped the table over, Danny ran back inside. She said quietly, "Bed time, love."

"They're so cute, Mum. Couldn't I have Lucky in bed with me tonight? I'll be careful with her, I promise!"

"No, love, leave her with her mother and her brothers and sisters. She's happier there. Now into the bathroom with you."

As soon as she heard water running in the bathroom, she went once again to the two rifles, checking that the safeties were off, then stood quietly in front of the wood stove, staring into the flames through the grill.

He was seeing things in this dream which weren't possible. He was watching a woman prepare to commit

75

murder, he knew that, but his gentle loving mother was incapable of such an act. She'd put enough drugs into Danny's custard to kill him, but hadn't seen him tip most of it away, although he must have had enough in the little he'd ingested to affect him in some way. And Connie, fanatically safety conscious Connie, had loaded two rifles and left them lying around with the safety catches off. He knew his mother would never do such a thing. In realising this, he understood that the dream was nonsense. Whatever else happened now, it wasn't important because it wasn't believable. And he must wake up soon. Dreams don't last forever.

Dan was beginning to chill on the shed roof. The last of the afternoon light was disappearing and an early evening dampness was setting in. He was tired. He took his eyes off the kitchen window and looked behind him. The orchard was gloomy in the darkening shadows. He wondered what would happen if he let himself drift off to sleep. Can a person sleep inside a dream?

A new noise caught his attention and he brought his gaze back to the house. Alec was standing at this end of the veranda, only a few feet away. Dan tensed. Alec proceeded to empty his bladder onto the daisy bushes, the cigarette hanging limply from his mouth, his drunken gaze looking at nothing in particular. When he had finished, he went back inside. Mum was sitting at the table with a perfect stillness that went unnoticed. Alec went to the fridge for another bottle of beer.

Danny came into the room in his pyjamas, rubbing his eyes and yawning. Connie suddenly pulled him to her and held him tight. Alec ignored them and went outside again.

The boy squirmed listlessly inside his mother's embrace. "I'm tired, Mum, I'm going to bed."

"Yes, Danny love, yes, but let's have a cuddle first. OK?" There was a desperate edge to her voice.

Danny leaned his head into her and yawned noisily.

"You know I've always loved you, Danny. You know you've always come first with me. You know that, don't you?"

"Mmmm."

"You know I'd never let you suffer, never let anyone hurt you. You know that …" She couldn't go on. Danny seemed unaware of her torment.

"Tired, Mum."

"Alright love, I'll come and tuck you in." She guided the boy into the passage.

Dan shifted his attention to his old bedroom as he saw the light come on. Danny flopped onto the bed. Connie removed his slippers, slipped him under the bedclothes and lay down beside him, carefully pulling her hair across to cover most of her face. Danny rolled over and closed his eyes, his mother enfolding him in her arms, silent tears wetting the pillowcase under her cheek. His breathing deepened. He was asleep.

The bang of the kitchen door made her jump. "Con!" She sat up shakily and wiped her eyes. Then she leaned down and kissed Danny's forehead, kissed his cheeks and his chin, the top of his head, kissed him until she heard Alec's harsh cry again, "Con! Where the fuck are you?"

She rose slowly, gave Danny a look full of despair and longing, and went into the kitchen.

Dan shifted his weight until he had a clear view into the kitchen again. Alec was at the fridge door. As Connie entered the room, he said, "Jeez, Con, you're fucking hopeless. I'm outa beer. I told you to keep the fridge stocked. Christ, I'll have to get it myself." He slammed the fridge door shut and turned to go into the laundry where the cartons of beer were stacked. As he did so, Connie bent quickly, picked up Alec's rifle and raised it, the barrel just inches from his face.

Alec stopped, shocked for a second, then threw his head back and laughed coarsely. "What's this? Trying to change my mind about tomorrow?" He reached forward to take the rifle from her, but she jumped back. She was shaking so badly that her finger kept slipping from the trigger. "Give me the gun or I'll give you a taste of what you deserve, you stupid fucking slut!"

She stepped back again, but kept the rifle aimed. "Christ, you're a waste of space, Con," he said with contempt. "You think you can frighten me with an unloaded rifle? You think anything you could do would frighten me?" Then he turned away as casually as if Connie wasn't there and began to walk towards the laundry. "Ah, what the fuck. I need a drink. You'll keep. I don't get you now, I'll sure as hell get you later."

Connie's eyes narrowed and she inhaled deeply, as if she was about to dive into water. She steadied herself, closed her eyes and pulled the trigger.

The bullet smashed into the back of Alec's head and exploded his face against the kitchen wall, the impact throwing him against the corner of the table which spun him around so that he landed backwards against the wall. At first his faceless body stayed erect, arms outstretched as if crucified, then he slumped to the floor, dragging a heavy smear of blood down the wall with him.

CHAPTER SEVEN

For a split second, Dan didn't register what he had seen, but then adrenalin poured through his veins like cold steel. He stumbled to his knees and moved backwards to climb down the ladder, but misjudged and knocked the ladder away with his foot.

Connie was still standing in the firing position, oblivious to Dan's noisy attempts to get off the roof. She remained unmoving for a second, then the rifle slowly slid from her fingers to land on the floor. Her trembling arms fell heavily to her side, her battered face twisted with emotion and she broke into loud sobs.

Then she bent down to take the second rifle and turned it to place the barrel in her mouth.

Dan screamed, "No! Mum! No!" He jumped to his feet and hurled himself off the roof, catching his shirt sleeve on the gutter and ripping part of it away. He landed squarely on the damp soil. With a couple of strides he was on the veranda and through the kitchen door.

Connie's hand reached for the trigger, her eyes closed, the tears streaming down the sides of her face. She was shaking so much that the barrel clattered against her teeth. Dan dived across the room with arms outstretched and flung the rifle away from them both, hitting her nose and cutting her lip in the process. The rifle clattered to the floor by the passage door without discharging.

"What are you doing, Mum?" he cried, then glanced back to see Alec's body on the floor. "What have you done?" He turned back to see Connie's eyes turn to white as she passed out and caught her as she tilted backwards. He held her and burst into hot, frightened tears.

It no longer mattered whether this was a dream or not. What he felt now was real. He held his despairing mother in his arms and felt the heat and sweat of her body. He saw his dead father and smelled the cloying scent of warm blood and raw flesh. The room was splattered with blood and a pool of it was spreading around his father. He howled into the dusk, "Mum! Mum! What have you done?"

The woman in his arms trembled as she returned to consciousness, called back by something in his voice that her deep subconscious recognised. She looked up into his tear-ravaged face and stiffened, her eyes wide with new terror. "No, Mum, it's alright, it's alright. It's me, it's Dan, your Dan. Mum, I'm Danny." He held her tight, afraid of what she might do if he let her go.

A noise behind him suddenly shifted his universe sideways again. Danny was in the passage behind him. He was in the passage behind himself.

Suddenly, Dan knew what he had to do.

He twisted around a little so that he was placed squarely between Connie and young Danny. He spoke urgently through his sobs. "Mum, I know you don't believe me. You think I'm a crazy stranger, but that's Danny coming up the passage now, that's me thirty years ago. I was woken by the noise and I came up the passage to see what it was. Watch, now, watch, Mum."

Gripping his mother to him as she tried fruitlessly to push him away, Dan twisted a little more so that she could see past his shoulder. He felt her freeze in his arms. "He's seeing us now, he's seeing the blood coming from your nose and your mouth where I knocked you. Now he's looking over at Dad. He's seeing Dad and thinking I killed him. He's looking back at us and thinking I'm trying to kill you. Now he's seeing his rifle on the floor, he's reaching for it, he's raising it but he's groggy with those sleeping tablets you put in the custard. He can't focus properly, but he's raising the rifle and he'll fire because he believes it is the only chance there is to save you. The bullet will hit me first, it will pass through my arm and hit you just here," he touched her just below the shoulder, "and lodge in the muscle. The recoil will hit him in the face and break his nose. It will knock him off his feet and he'll pass out …"

They both flinched as the rifle discharged and the bullet tore through Dan's arm and into Connie's flesh. She cried out with the pain. Then they heard Danny fall. Dan released his mother and she ran to the boy, screaming, "Danny! Danny!"

"He's alright, Mum, he'll be alright. Look, I'm here, I survived, I'm alright."

Ignoring Dan, she knelt next to the boy. "Danny. Wake up, Danny. Oh god, what have I done?" She looked up at Dan and cried hysterically, "We have to help him! We have to keep him awake!"

"He'll be alright."

"No. You don't understand. You don't know what I did. Help him!" She slipped her good arm under Danny

81

and pulled him into a fierce embrace, all thought of herself gone.

Dan said quietly, "You crushed sleeping tablets and put them in his custard, enough to kill a full grown man, but you didn't see what he did. I saw it. When you were getting the cream for Dad, when your back was turned, he tipped it down the sink because he wanted to go to Lucky. He wouldn't have had enough to do any damage, but he'll sleep through to the middle of tomorrow."

Connie looked up sharply at his words. "How do you know that?"

"Because I've been watching you all afternoon from the roof of the garden shed. I saw everything."

"You saw everything?" A shock wave of understanding passed across her features. "Then ... then that means that if you hadn't stopped me, he would have woken tomorrow and found us ... me and Alec ... here ... in the kitchen."

"Yes."

"Oh god." Connie dissolved into deep rocking sobs, her face buried in Danny's hair as she cried over and over, "What have I done? What have I done?"

It was unbearable to watch. He breathed deep and hard to stem the flow of his own tears. He had to get control of himself.

Dan felt the wound in his arm searing with heat and pain. It was exposed where the piece of shirtsleeve had torn away. He pulled a handkerchief from his pocket and covered the wound, suddenly feeling weak and dizzy. He knew he was in shock. So was his mother. He flopped onto a chair and rested his head in his hands, the tears slowing as he fought to stay conscious.

They stayed like that for a moment, unable to think, unable to move, until Dan heard Connie's sobs change to a strange wheezing sound. He looked up. She was staring across the room at Alec, her eyes glassy, not wanting to see, but unable to look anywhere else. "I have to get out … get out … can't stay here …" She began to struggle with Danny's weight as she tried to get to her feet.

Instinctively, Dan went to her aid. As painful as his arm was, the wound was superficial, the bullet having only scraped underneath the surface of the bicep, so he was able to use both arms to lift Danny and take him outside. Connie followed, her breath coming in short, sharp rasps behind him. He stopped on the veranda, uncertain what to do next, his mother bumping into him with unseeing eyes. He knew she was hyperventilating and sensed another faint coming on.

Quickly laying Danny against the wall, he took his mother firmly and sat her on the edge of the veranda. Gently pushing her head between her knees, he said, "Deep slow breaths, Mum, deep slow breaths. You're going to be alright, I promise you, everything will be alright." He went on talking softly with soothing words until he heard her breathing stabilise. She leaned her elbows on her knees and rested her head in her hands with eyes closed.

The light from the kitchen cast a dim glow around them. Beyond that circle of light, all was pitch black under a moonless cloudy sky. The air was still and damp with the promise of more rain.

Danny rolled over onto his back behind them and began to snore. Connie looked up. "He'll get cold. I need to …"

"I'll get it," Dan cut in, and rose to go back into the house. He reeled back as he circled the kitchen table, seeing the blood splattered across the walls, the ceiling, the table and the floor. He tried not to look at his father's body, but his peripheral vision took in the faceless horror a few feet away. A new odour of urine and faeces was mingling with the scent of fresh blood as the lifeless body shed its waste. Dan covered his nose and mouth with his hand and went to the linen cupboard in the passage. Reaching in, he retrieved a grey army blanket for Danny, then hesitated as he thought it through and took another two blankets for himself and Connie and a large towel.

Back on the veranda, he bent over Danny to wrap the grey blanket around him securely, rolling it at the end to make a pillow. Then he gently dropped a blanket of coloured crocheted squares over Connie's shoulders. She pulled it tight around her, watching Dan as she did so. He dropped the third blanket next to her and headed towards the kitchen. "What are you doing?" she whispered hoarsely.

"Covering Dad's face," he answered simply, holding the towel up.

Connie gulped with new tears and nodded her consent.

Dan walked towards his father's body with averted eyes, taking care not to slip in the blood. He held the towel out and dropped it carefully over the head and torso, retching as he did so. Looking down to satisfy himself that the body was covered, he backed away quickly. He registered that his Nikes were leaving a trail of bloodied footprints and went back to his mother.

Connie hadn't moved. He said, "It's done," and she threw up into the daisy bush next to her. Dan sat with her, holding her by the shoulders until she stopped. He pulled the other blanket around his shoulders against the night chill. They were both trembling badly.

"What do I do now?" Connie asked helplessly into the night, the tears unchecked.

"For a start, we have to stop that bleeding," Dan responded, indicating the blood running down her arm and dripping from her fingertips. He looked down at his own arm, removing the handkerchief to inspect the wound. The bleeding had congealed and stopped. It burned with pain, but he knew he was alright.

Connie, ever practical by nature, looked at her wound and said, "There are bandages in the first aid kit. It's …" She looked back at the kitchen and shook her head. "I can't go in there. I can't ever go in there again."

"I'll go."

Dan averted his eyes, but it was easier this time with Alec's face covered. Reaching up quickly into the cupboard next to the wood stove, he took the old cake tin that held the makeshift first aid kit. The warmth from the stove was welcome. Suddenly, he felt cold, exhausted, hungry and very thirsty. On impulse, he pulled down the large teapot from the mantle above the stove and quickly filled it with simmering water from the blackened water fountain on the side of the stove, then took the tea and sugar canisters, tipped some of both into the teapot, opened the fridge for milk and added some to the mixture, gathered the biscuit tin from the cupboard above the sink, collected two cups from the cup hooks and carried them outside.

Dan put the teapot, cups and biscuits between them. Connie, still weeping, was looking at him strangely. "How did you know where everything was? I didn't tell you."

"I know where everything is because this used to be my home." He poured tea and handed her a cup. "Drink this, it'll help with the shock." He gulped down his own cupful, then poured another.

"That's nonsense. Tell me how you know." She brought the tea to her swollen lips with shaking hands and sipped carefully.

Dan wolfed down a couple of biscuits, swiftly finished the second cup of tea and opened the first aid kit. He tipped a little Dettol onto cotton wool and began dabbing at her bullet wound, his own hands shaking to match his mother's.

"Does this hurt, Mum?"

"No. It's numb. How do you know? Tell me. And why do you keep calling me Mum?"

He took a deep breath. "Because I'm Dan, Mum, I'm Daniel James Campbell, your Dan."

"That's ridiculous. That's my son over there and his name is Daniel James Averill. You told me your name was Hamish Walsh."

"I'm Danny, Mum, just thirty years older."

"That's mad talk. You're frightening me. Stop it."

"I'm sorry, I don't mean to frighten you. Maybe it is mad talk. I don't understand any of this. I thought I was having a dream, but it's too real and ... and it makes sense of something I was never able to make sense of before. Maybe I've gone back through time, maybe I've lost my mind, I don't know."

Dan could feel the bullet under the surface just below her shoulder bone and remembered seeing the white surgical scar only a few days ago. Mum always wore sleeves because she was self-conscious of the scar. But right now, all he could see was blood appearing as quickly as he wiped it away. He remembered Mum telling him once that her arm often ached because the bullet had damaged blood vessels and nerves. He knew it was a serious wound.

He glanced up to see her fear-filled eyes. "I haven't hurt you or Danny, have I? And I won't, I promise you. If I hadn't been here, you'd be dead and what would have happened to Danny?" He looked back at the wound and added quietly, "What would have happened to me?" He let the question sit with her while he worked at the wound.

"But you aren't Danny. Who are you? And why did you come back?"

"I came back to see if you were alright. You and Danny. I didn't know Dad was like that …"

"Stop talking like that, please."

"I didn't know about Dad, you see," he persisted, "I didn't remember him like that. It was a shock and I had to know if you were OK." He lifted her limp arm a little to wrap the bandage around it.

"Stop lying to me. Who are you really? And why us?"

"Oh Mum, how can I explain this? I'm your son. Thirty years ago on my eleventh birthday, Dad was murdered by a stranger. Around every birthday, I get depressed. I don't cope well at all and my wife told me I had to deal with it. So I came back – we live in England now – I came back with you to confront my memories.

You, the fifty eight year old you, is back at the hotel in town waiting for me. I came out alone because I thought it would be too hard for you. I got to the crest of the hill and either I fainted and this is a dream, or I finally lost my mind completely, or I passed through some sort of time warp, but here I am. And as unbelievable as it sounds, I'm the stranger I saw thirty years ago. But I'm your son, too. I don't understand any of this, but it feels as real as anything I've felt in my whole life."

He raised his eyes, their faces only inches apart. She said, "Your eyes are like Danny's."

"That's because I am Danny." They spoke softly in the cocoon of dim light, conscious of the sleeping child behind them.

"You know I can't believe such a story. It's impossible. But, well, you do sort of look like Danny. Are you a relative?"

"I can't tell you anything other than I'm Danny." He finished wrapping the arm and secured the bandage with a safety pin. "Look, thirty years from now, you'll be waiting for me at the hotel. Irene – remember Irene from school? Irene runs the hotel now, she'll be there with you. You'll be worried about me because I told you I'd be back by lunch time. You need something," he looked around him, "something from this moment, something to keep and give to me when I get back. Something that will prove to you it was me here, something that can convince me that I really was here." He saw the top of the fridge through the kitchen window. "I know."

He rose and went inside, returning with the camera in his hand. "I'll take a photo of myself, Mum. No, better still, I'll take one of both of us. Here, like this." He held the camera high before them, leaned in to her until their heads were touching and pressed the button. The flash made them both jump. "There are three photos left. I'll take another." He turned the camera on Connie and snapped before she had time to respond. Then he took another of Danny snoring on the veranda. One left. It had to be a good one.

Connie was watching him like the madman she believed him to be.

Proof. That was what he was wanting. His arm twinged as he looked back at Danny. He needed a photo of the three of them together.

Going to one of the chairs, he carefully placed the camera on it so that he could see Danny and Connie through the viewfinder. He pressed a button and quickly moved to kneel between the two of them.

"What are you doing?"

"This camera has an eight second delay button on it. I used it all the time to take photos of me and Lucky. Watch, the flash will go off …" he paused, "… now!"

Dan got up and handed the camera to Connie. "Get this developed and hold on to the photos. But wait awhile. Wait until the police have finished out here. There's a second cartridge somewhere, isn't there? I heard you tell Danny."

"Yes. In the kitchen drawer."

Dan found it. He replaced the finished film with the new cartridge. "Hide this, Mum," he instructed, holding up the finished film. "Keep it safe until you can get it developed, but don't get it developed anywhere locally. Wait until you are in England. Then keep these photos locked away until you come back in thirty years."

Connie was shaking her head slowly in disbelief.

"Please, Mum. Just do it. Tell me you'll do it."

Connie nodded uncertainly. Dan could see that she was too afraid of his strange behaviour to argue. He looked around him. "Where to hide the film, that's the next thing. Somewhere the police won't find it, but somewhere easy for you to get it when you can." A metal boot scraper next to the veranda steps caught his attention. He turned it upside down. A metal rod ran from one side to the other under the angled scraping surface to give it strength. He slid the cartridge under the rod. It was a perfect fit and invisible from above.

"Don't forget where it is," he added as he looked up. Connie nodded weakly, then sighed and slumped forward, her eyes unseeing, blood running freely from under the bandage. He leapt to her side, drew her back and wrapped her in his arms. "Mum? Are you alright? Oh god oh Mum. Come back, come back."

Dan heard a deep sighing breath as she came to. Cradling her limp body like a child's, he began to rock to and fro, repeating over and over, "It's finished, it's behind you, it'll be alright, I'll look after you, I promise. I'll never leave you, it'll be alright, I promise"

She didn't pull away. It was the first comfort of any sort she'd experienced in a long time, even if it was coming from a madman. Her tears wet his shirt front.

Dan felt hot stickiness on his hand. Blood was pooling on the veranda between them. "We have to get you to hospital."

"Hospital?" She looked up at him, her voice weak, but insistent. "No hospital. That would mean police, they'd put me in jail and what would happen to Danny?

No." She flinched with pain as the numbness in her arm began to wear off.

"You're not going to jail, Mum. I know everything that is going to happen for the next thirty years. You're going to be fine." It sounded ridiculous.

"No, I'm not going to be fine." Hysteria crept into her voice. "I murdered my husband. How can I be fine?"

"Because you'll tell them that I did it. You'll tell them that a stranger came to the house during the day, that Dad was suspicious of him and sent him away and that he came back that night and killed Dad. You'll tell them that the stranger beat you, that's why your face is all messed up."

"They'd never believe such a story." She tried to pull away from him. "Oh god, I'm dizzy. I feel sick." She leaned over and vomited into the bushes again. Dan held her by the shoulders until the spasm was over, then pulled her against him. Clammy sweat glistened on her skin as she leaned in to him. He could feel the energy draining out of her.

"We've got to get you to help now."

She shook her head and whispered despairingly, "I can't drive like this. Oh god, what will I do?"

"I'll drive," Dan said on impulse, impelled by the sight of his mother sinking fast. "The station wagon. Where are the keys?"

"In the ignition." Of course. He'd forgotten that thirty years ago, people left their doors unlocked at night and the keys in their cars. He lay Connie on her side and made his way through the dark to the shed where the station wagon and the ute were parked. The dogs, locked away for the night in the neighbouring shed, barked furiously.

Dan backed the station wagon out, switched on the headlights and turned towards the house. As he pulled up next to the veranda, the headlights shone brightly in through the open kitchen door and his heart began to thump.

Alec was caught in the beam of light under the table. The towel had become saturated with blood and the heaviness of it had dragged it down to partly reveal the open gash of flesh and bone. Dan opened the car door and vomited into the grass. He waited until it passed, then turned the car back to face the other way. He didn't want his mother to have that image in her head. He would have to deal with his own memory of it later.

He went to her. "I feel very strange," she said feebly. The sight of her frightened him. He lifted her and placed her carefully on the front seat. She sagged across the bench seat. He went back for Danny and lay him across the back seat. Danny continued to snore, oblivious to the drama unfolding around him.

The sentinel gums on the track loomed white and ghostly in the circle of the headlights, making the night beyond empty black upon empty black. Turning onto the road, he reached down in the dimness to touch Connie's cold, clammy face. He heard her murmur. "Is Danny alright?"

She sounded far away. He wanted to keep her talking, to know she was still with him. "Can't you hear him snoring? I didn't know I snored, although Trish says I do sometimes."

"Trish?"

"My wife. Your daughter-in-law. The mother of your two grandsons, Hamish and Angus."

Connie didn't respond at first.

"Mum? Mum!"

Then she whispered with sad resignation, "That can never be. I will spend the rest of my life in jail and who knows what will become of Danny."

"Mum, I'm going to tell you what will happen. To you and to Danny. Are you listening?"

She tried to raise her head but flopped back onto the seat.

Dan slowed down, reached across and pulled her up until her head rested on his shoulder. He kept his arm around her. "Here's how it will go. You'll be in hospital tonight. First an operation on your arm, then about a week in hospital. I remember that because they let me stay with you. Someone seemed to understand that we shouldn't be separated after what we'd been through. Then the Taylors will come to take us both to stay with them because no one will expect you to go back to the house after what happened. The Taylors will arrange for some neighbours to help clean and pack up before we go to England. Although," he added, remembering the film cartridge, "you'll need to retrieve the film before someone else finds it. Don't forget, it's under the boot scraper, Mum, under the boot scraper."

He paused as he manoeuvred around a tight bend in the road. "We'll stay with the Taylors until harvest time, then the whole district will join together to help us get the harvest in and the sheep sheared. Everything that Dad never did for you will be done by kind hearted neighbours. It will be a good harvest and wool prices are still holding. Then a letter will arrive from your aunt in England, Grandma's sister, saying that she's ill and doesn't have long to live. She'll ask you to come to England to take over the pub where she and Grandma were born because she's leaving it to you in her will. The next day, the Taylors will make you an offer on the farm. It'll be a good offer, Mum. It's the last really good season this district will see for the next thirty years. There will be several severe droughts, wool prices will drop, everything will change. I know you don't believe it now, but this whole district will be a desert landscape in thirty years. You have to take the offer and go to England."

"I don't know anything about running a pub in England. All I know is the farm."

"You'll learn, Mum, you'll learn. And you'll meet Terry, he's a school headmaster, a wonderful man, and life will be very very good for you. You'll marry him."

"Stop. That's pure nonsense. None of that can happen."

"But it will."

"But it can't." She struggled with the next words. "My fingerprints are on the rifle and Danny saw everything."

Dan replied thoughtfully, "I should have wiped your prints off the rifle."

"And someone will see you driving me into town. Everyone knows this car. Someone will see."

Dan stopped the car, turned on the interior light and looked down at his mother. Her breathing was shallow and her skin pasty white. "Yes," he said slowly, "you're right. I haven't thought this through properly." They were silent for a moment. Then, "No-one would ever believe you could drive all the way into town, not the way you are. No." He rested his chin on the top of her head. "But they might believe you could drive to the nearest neighbour for help. Strange, I never thought to ask you how you got to hospital that night – this night. The one detail I never asked you about. It's your right arm that is injured, you can steer and change gears with your left arm. Let me think."

He stroked her hair tenderly, knowing he had to get her to help quickly, but needing this moment to decide how to go about it. The crocheted blanket had slipped from her shoulders. As he pulled it around her, he said, "I know you don't believe I'm your Danny, but think about this. This blanket. Grandma made it. I know that because I was home from school with the flu when I was about eight years old. It was hot inside the house, so you took me outside to sit on the veranda. You made me hot lemon and honey. I was shaking with fever, so you brought this blanket out and put it around me, just like I'm doing for you now. And you told me that Grandma had made this when she was in hospital. You'd just married Dad and you were pregnant with me. Grandma was dying of cancer and she knew she wouldn't live to see her grandchild born, so she made this blanket for me. She told you that she'd chosen the colours of the farm. White for the sheep's wool, gold for the ripe wheat, green for the new spring grass, blue for the big sky and red for the fire that warmed the kitchen on a cold winter's night."

Connie struggled to look up at him. "No one but my Danny could know that. He told you, didn't he? You know my Danny?"

"No, Mum, I am your Danny. You took this blanket to England with you and Trish, my wife Trish, made it into a quilt for our bed. It's one of my most precious possessions and every night when I go to bed, I remember that day on the veranda and what the colours mean."

Connie whispered hoarsely, "It's not possible." Her head fell weakly against Dan. "I don't know what to think. I'm so scared."

"Don't be scared. I'll take care of everything. I have to go back to the house. The police said the stranger had cleaned up after himself. He went back after you were gone to clean up anything that might identify him. It has to look that way to the police, doesn't it? They aren't to know that my fingerprints are Danny's fingerprints, and my blood is Danny's blood. They simply have to find nothing of the stranger. Except …" He looked down at his shoes. "… they found shoe prints, didn't they, but it didn't help them. They said the prints were clear but couldn't be identified, that they were possibly foreign." Suddenly, he remembered something. "Huh. Two years ago, when they reopened the case for DNA testing, they said that the evidence had been tampered with. They found prints for Nike cross-trainers that hadn't existed thirty years ago."

Connie looked at him with confusion. Nothing he was saying made sense.

His thoughts were racing as he planned ahead. He started the car again. "OK. Here's what we have to do. The Taylors are away but the Perry's should be home. They're another fifteen minutes down the road. I'll turn the lights off, get as close as I safely can, then stop far enough away so their dogs won't start up. I'll put you in the driver's seat, alright Mum?" She nodded weakly. "I'll get you into first gear, then I'll jump out. You can make it

96

to their front gate, stop and toot the horn until they come out. They're good people, they'll take care of you."

They drove in silence for a few moments, then Dan added, as if to himself, "Should take me about an hour to get back to the house. That'll give me plenty of time to arrange things for the police."

"But Danny saw you."

"It will all fit in with what Danny saw, Mum, I promise you."

Distant lights pierced the darkness ahead. Dan switched off the headlights and slowed down. He could just make out the fence line on either side of the road and used that as a guide.

Connie whispered, "How do you know that?"

"Because, as I keep telling you, I'm Danny. What Danny saw are my own memories."

Connie tilted her head a little to look up. "OK, if you're Danny, tell me what you saw."

"I saw …" The old confusion suddenly returned. "I saw the stranger – me – fighting with you in the kitchen."

"Why did you wake up in the first place?"

"I heard a noise, a loud noise, probably the shot you fired."

Dan stopped the car, turned on the interior light and looked down into his mother's deeply troubled eyes. The sight made him flinch inwardly. "I had trouble waking up. I guess I know why now. The sleeping tablets in the custard."

Connie looked away.

"Mum, it wasn't your fault. You have to understand that. Dad was – he was a monster!" He felt tears well up. It would take awhile to get his head around the

97

revelations of this day. "He pushed you past the point of endurance until you could only see one way out for both of us." He tightened his arm around her. "You believed you were sparing me from what Dad had planned for me, I understand that. You wanted the nightmare to end for both of us and there was only one way to do that. You'd already tried to leave. I remember those two trips to the coast and Dad coming to take us home. But I don't remember the beatings."

"I always got Danny away before Alec started in on me."

"But your face and the bruises, why didn't I see them?"

"That's why I keep my hair long, so I can hide behind it, and I always wear sleeves to cover the bruises."

"Does anyone else know what he's like? The neighbours, the people in town?"

"I've tried to cover for him because of Danny and I stay away from people until I heal. But he isn't very popular with most people."

"Yes. I can see why. People aren't fools." Dan withdrew his arm from around her shoulders. "Come on, Mum, see if you can slide across here." Opening the car door, he stepped out and helped her across until she was in the driver's seat. The effort cost her dearly and she rested her head against the steering wheel for a moment.

She whispered breathlessly, "What else did Danny see?"

He propped her up a little, turned off the interior light, reached across to put the gearstick into neutral and started the motor. Cool darkness wrapped itself around them, turning their faces into grey masks.

"I saw you struggling with the stranger, but he wouldn't let you go. I looked across and saw Dad. It was like a punch in the guts. I felt sick and dizzy. Then I saw the rifle, my rifle on the floor in front of me. I picked it up, but it felt so heavy I could hardly hold it. The safety catch was off. I hoped it was loaded. I knew I had one chance to fire, one chance to save you. Then I saw …"

Dan hesitated. What was it that he'd seen that had confused him so much for the past thirty years? He squatted next to Connie and looked up at her. "I saw your face. That was it. I saw your face looking past the stranger's shoulder. He was talking to you, but you weren't struggling with him any longer. You were listening to him and watching me. And you weren't afraid of him. I couldn't make sense of what I was seeing. You should have been screaming and fighting the stranger. You should have been yelling out to me to run away, but instead you were very still. You were both very still. He was talking quietly and you were watching me. You were … you were strangely curious. You were watching me while the stranger was talking to you and you were curious."

Dan shook his head as the memories fell into place. "Now I understand. When I saw that look on your face, that curious look, I hesitated. For a second, I didn't know whether I should fire or not, but then I felt myself sliding into a faint and my finger squeezed the trigger without me making the decision. I heard it roar in my head, I felt the recoil hit me squarely in the face, and then nothing. Nothing until I woke up in hospital with a broken nose."

He felt a soft touch on his cheek and looked up. Connie had twisted around a little and stroked his face gently with her good hand. "You can't be Danny, even with that story, but you're kind. I think you're crazy, but you're kind. I don't believe you are capable of hurting anyone and … and you're the first person to show me any real kindness since my parents died. Thank you." She leaned against the steering wheel again.

Dan looked at the blood stained bandage on her arm. "We have to take the bandage off," he said, and removed it. "Can't have anyone asking how you managed to bandage your own arm in the state you're in." He tucked it into his shorts pocket. Blood ran down her arm freely to soak her shorts. Her t-shirt was soaked with her own and Danny's blood. There seemed to be a lot of it.

"Can you make it to the Perry's, Mum?" He looked down the road at the distant lights.

"I'll try," she whispered. "It's not far now."

Dan shut the door, wiped it with a clean corner of his shirt, went around to the other side and got in next to her. He spent a moment wiping the steering wheel, gearstick and door handles clean. "Have you got the story straight, Mum? Tell me what you're going to say to the police."

"I'm not sure."

He heard the frightened catch in her voice. "Mum, listen to me. Listen carefully." He leaned toward her intently. "You tell them that I came to the house saying that I'd run out of petrol on the road. That's true, so it's easy for you. When the police find the full jerrycan by the front gate, they'll know that I was lying. They'll know just from that discovery that my motives were sinister. You say that the stranger was nice to you, but that Dad was suspicious from the beginning. Tell them that he ordered the stranger off the farm at gunpoint. Make Dad sound like the hero in this. It's important, Mum. Then say that you spent the afternoon in the house, just doing normal stuff. Danny will back you up. He didn't see the beating Dad gave you and he was so wrapped up in Lucky and his new rifle that he didn't notice your injuries. Tell them that you gave Danny one of your sleeping tablets, the last one in the bottle, because he was so wired up from the excitement of the day that you knew he wouldn't sleep. That'll explain his drugged state. Then say that the stranger came back after tea, burst into the kitchen and shot Dad. Say he'd used Dad's own rifle. Then he threatened to shoot you with Danny's rifle, but you tried to fight him off and he'd dropped it. Danny came up the passage, picked up his rifle and shot the stranger. The stranger ran off. Say that you managed to get Danny out to the car and drove to the Perry's for help. Can you remember that, Mum, can you remember the details?"

Connie was listening to him with her head resting on the steering wheel. He heard her say faintly, "Yes. I'll remember."

"Good. We have to go, Mum, we have to go now." He moved closer and slid his leg next to hers so that his foot rested on the clutch. "Just work the accelerator, Mum, I'll do the clutch and gearstick." He put the car into first and let out the clutch. "More accelerator. That's it. A bit more now. Good. When you get close, turn off the motor and let it roll to a stop – you're not strong enough to work the brake pedal – and hit the horn." He leaned across and kissed her swollen cheek. "I love you Mum. I understand and I don't blame you. You are innocent." He heard her suck in her breath with emotion.

They moved slowly down the road until they were no more than a few hundred yards from the Perry's house. Dan was about to open the door and jump out when a final thought stopped him. He turned to Connie and said urgently, "One more thing, Mum. Danny thinks his father is a hero. Please, please let him keep that illusion. Let him have the next thirty years believing his father was a good man, that his father loved him and was murdered by a mad stranger, that he saved you by shooting the stranger and that his childhood before that was a good one. It would destroy him to think any different. It will be hard for you, I understand that now, but he needs that illusion. Please, promise me you'll do that?"

Connie turned slowly to look at him. She waited a moment before answering, then whispered, "Alright. I promise." She looked away. "We're getting close."

Dan saw the lights ahead, opened the door, took a deep breath and leapt out. He landed squarely on his backside, quickly got to his feet and watched the car approach the house up ahead. He could hear dogs barking. A veranda light came on just as Connie hit the horn.

CHAPTER EIGHT

Dan turned and started to run. He figured that by the time the Perry family got Connie into town, he'd be back at the farm. Then the police would be contacted and drive out as soon as they'd spoken to Connie. A couple of hours, maybe three. He'd have plenty of time to arrange things and get away.

Then what? If indeed he had travelled back in time, would he be stuck in this time forever? Would Mum be waiting at the hotel for a son who had ceased to exist in her own time? Would he have to find a way to live in this time again, but as an adult, with himself as a child somewhere else on the planet?

It was too hard to imagine, and anyway, there was much to do in the here and now, whatever that really was. He would worry later about it later.

It felt good to be running. He picked up the pace and revelled in the rush of endorphins. His head cleared and he began to plan what he needed to do.

The night was cool and the sweet smell of the Australian bush after rain filled his nostrils. His eyes adjusted quickly to the darkness and the landscape rolled away from him in shades of grey and silver. A fine misty rain began to fall and, by the time he reached the farm gates, it was steady thrumming rain.

Stopping to rest against one of the stone pillars, he suddenly remembered the day after the murder, lying in a bed near Mum in hospital, hearing the police telling her that it had rained heavily the night before, washing away all evidence of the stranger outside the house, except for a pair of shoe prints. Mum hadn't remembered the rain. She was already on her way to hospital by then and barely conscious. Realising that Danny could hear the conversation, a nurse came and took him outside in a wheelchair. He'd heard nothing more.

The jerrycan of fuel was where he had left it earlier that day with the water bottle. Dan bent to wipe underneath the handle and the bottom of the jerrycan. The rain had already washed the rest clean. He held the water bottle, the biscuit and snack bar wrappings and wondered what to do with them. They were not a part of this era and needed disposal. He could throw them out into the paddock, but if the police conducted a thorough search, they would be found.

The two stone pillars that formed the gateway loomed over him. When he was a boy, he'd often climbed one or the other to sit on until the school bus came. He remembered that there were some loose stones at the back of one of the pillars which he'd had to avoid when he climbed. Running his hands over the stones until he found one that moved, he jiggled it hard. It came away. Behind it were more stones. He pulled at them until he'd removed several and made a hole inside the pillar. Pushing the bottle and wrappings inside, he began cramming stones back into the hole, then remembered the bloodied bandage in his pocket and added that to the stash. The outer stone still felt loose, so he scooped up a handful of wet soil and used it like mortar to stick it back in place. In the dark, it looked as it should. He turned and continued to run.

At the crest of the hill, Dan paused and looked down at the glow of lights from the house. It looked soft and gentle in the rain, so warm and inviting, with no hint of the horror inside.

Rain poured from him in rivulets as he ran the last few yards to the house. Standing on the veranda to catch his breath, he shook the wetness from his head and looked down. Water collected in clear puddles around his shoes. The rain had washed him clean of blood.

First things first. Dan removed his saturated shoes, socks, shorts and shirt and left them spread out on the veranda steps. In just his underpants, he collected the teapot and cups, the first aid kit and the dirty cotton balls.

Standing in the kitchen doorway, he took stock. He'd left bloodied shoe prints all over the kitchen floor and the veranda. Thinking it through, he figured it would be a mixture of his own blood and Connie's blood from their rifle wounds as well as Alec's blood which had splattered around the room. He'd have to make it look like he, the stranger, had cleaned up his own blood. That had to be the motive for coming back. Blood and finger prints. It didn't matter if he missed a bit, because it would be Danny's blood and fingerprints, but it did matter where they were found.

A small pool of blood from Danny's broken nose lay next to his discharged rifle in the entrance to the passage. That needed to stay as it was.

Dan's stomach tightened as he looked across at Alec. The blood-heavy towel lay in a heap in the dead man's lap. A pool of black blood formed a neat ring around the crumpled body. He'd have to remove the towel, but the blood pool should remain unbroken. He looked away, not sure how to go about it. Where to hide the towel?

He suddenly remembered his childhood treasure trove and a feeling of calm flooded through him. He could do this. He knew he could because he was on home territory. There wasn't anything about this place he didn't know intimately. As he thought it and felt it, he knew Mum's future depended on what he did here. What the police found had to fit with what he remembered being told about the stranger.

The stranger had killed Dad. Mum and Danny fled a scene of bloodied mayhem, but when the police arrived, they found all evidence of the stranger gone. They found a scrupulously cleaned house with only Dad's body left as evidence of what had happened.

And a pair of shoe prints somewhere outside, somewhere not affected by the rain. The only trace left of the stranger's existence.

It occurred to Dan now that, without any evidence at all of the stranger's presence, the police might have suspected Connie after all. He'd never had that impression as a child. Mum had been treated very kindly and without suspicion by all concerned. Had something else happened that he hadn't been told about? Something that had convinced the police and everyone else that the stranger did indeed exist?

It was possible. Dan was only eleven at the time and had lived inside his own grief-stricken world for a long time after Dad's death. There were probably many grown up things going on around him that he'd been unaware of. He would never know.

He'd have to work with what he did know. There was no other choice.

With the sound of the rain thundering on the iron roof above, he carefully dropped the collection of things from the veranda on to the table and walked quickly to Danny's bedroom. He retrieved the screwdriver from the bedside cabinet, lifted the rug and began working at one of the floorboards. This had been his secret place, no one else knew of it. The floorboard lifted and he reached in. A battered cake tin held the things that small boys treasure – a few shillings, a sling shot Mum had banned him from using, a Superman comic book and several Matchbox cars. Dan felt in around where the tin had been. There was room.

Going back to the kitchen, he took in a breath, held it and stepped forward to retrieve the bloodied towel with the end of the screwdriver. The stench was unbearable. He took it quickly to the floor cavity, dropped it in, used the screwdriver to push it back under the floor as far as he could, replaced the tin, floorboard and rug, wiped the screwdriver clean on his wet underpants, put it back in the bedside cabinet and ran from the room.

Outside, Dan retched and retched until he felt that there couldn't be anything left in his stomach to bring up. Then he stepped into the clean cold rain until the blood stain on his underpants washed away and he felt the control return. He hadn't finished yet.

Under the kitchen sink he found a pair of rubber gloves which he put on. He filled the sink with hot soapy water and began. Taking care not to look at Alec's body, he tidied the kitchen, washing, cleaning and putting things back where they belonged. Then he washed down every cupboard, handle, container, light switch and wall, except for the wall which Alec lay against. Looking up, he decided against washing the ceiling. Only his father's blood had made it that far. He emptied and cleaned the sink.

The cotton wool he'd used to clean Connie's wound remained. He thought for a moment, aware that the smell of the Dettol would alert anyone to their presence. Any evidence of Connie's wound being tended to wouldn't fit. The fire in the wood stove had burned down to glowing coals. Taking a small log from the wood basket next to the stove, he stoked the fire until it revived and tossed the cotton wool in, making sure it had burned away completely before closing the grate.

Next, the bloodied footprints.

Dan took care to step around Danny's blood on his way into the laundry. He looked back and saw that his damp bare feet were leaving marks on the floor. He'd need something to cover them. A pair of dirty socks lay on top of the laundry basket. They were Connie's. He pulled them on, then filled a bucket with hot water and disinfectant and began to mop the floor, being careful not to leave any footprints on the damp surface. He took the mop to the edge of the pool of blood around Alec, but no further, manoeuvred around Danny's blood and into the passage, then wiped down the linen cupboard doors.

The water in the bucket was black. Dan emptied and refilled it again, then went outside to wash down the veranda. Dipping a cloth into the bucket, he cleaned the chairs and table, the veranda posts and the architraves around the door. He was sure he hadn't missed anything. Tossing the water out into the garden, he threw the bucket into the rain and thrust the mop head into the mud. There would be nothing left for the police to find by the time they got to the farm. The rain was taking care of that.

It was done.

Standing on the veranda, he went over it in his mind. The stranger came to the house during the day on the pretence that his car had run out of fuel on the road. The police would find the jerrycan by the gate and know that couldn't have been the real motive, so the stranger became a man with malicious intent. Alec didn't like the look of him or the way he spoke to Connie, which would back the police's theory, and had ordered him off the farm at gunpoint. The stranger returned that night, watched the family from outside somewhere and waited for the right moment to enter the kitchen. The two loaded rifles were still lying against the wall next to the fridge. He'd taken the bigger rifle and shot Alec in the back of the head without warning. The stranger had then taken Danny's rifle and threatened Connie, but he'd dropped it in the doorway to the passage when Connie struggled with him. They didn't hear Danny coming down the passage. Danny saw them struggling, saw the rifle on the floor in front of him, reached for it, fired and the bullet passed through the stranger's arm and into Connie's. The stranger ran off. Connie got Danny into the car and left, but the stranger must have stayed close by, because after he saw them leave, he went back to remove all evidence of his presence.

It seemed to fit. The washed floors were dry. It was time to go. He pulled Connie's socks off and dressed quickly, then realised he should replace Connie's socks where he'd found them. Taking off his Nikes and shoving them into each side pocket, he walked back inside, his own socks leaving no marks on the clean floors. He dropped Connie's socks back onto the laundry basket and went outside.

The rain had stopped and all was silent.

Dan felt uneasy. There was something wrong. He knew it instinctively. He'd missed something. Then it came to him.

The shoe prints the police had found. That was it. He had to leave a clear set of shoe prints behind. But where?

They had to be outside the house. Maybe on the washed veranda? But that didn't seem right. Too contrived. The stranger had been thorough, he wouldn't wash the veranda then leave shoe prints on it. Maybe on the steps? The top step was a little more sheltered from the rain than the steps below it. No, it would be too obvious there. It had to look like it was missed in the clean up.

He looked around him, feeling more desperate by the minute. Spinning on his heel slowly, he looked for a logical place for a set of shoe prints that might get missed in the clean up. As his gaze passed across the kitchen door, he noticed something else that didn't ring true.

Alec's rifle. He'd cleaned it carefully and put it back where it had been on the floor. It wasn't consistent with the cover up he'd just completed. A murderous stranger would not have left it like that. He should have put it back next to the fridge, in keeping with the rest of the cleaning and tidying. Perhaps he should have done the same with Danny's blood and rifle?

Suddenly, he felt confused. He had to get this right. Should he leave Danny's rifle there, or clean it up and put it back next to the fridge as well? Where had they been found by the police? It was a detail he'd never thought to ask. He only remembered that the police had found the rifles in the kitchen, the big rifle wiped of prints, the smaller rifle with Danny's and Mum's prints all over it.

Why would the stranger clean one rifle and not the other? It didn't matter that Danny's and Mum's prints were the only ones on his rifle. They had both handled it during the day. What mattered was that the stranger was supposed to have threatened Mum with it, then dropped it, so of course the stranger's prints should have been on it, too. He would have cleaned that as well. Had it only been partly cleaned? And why?

Dan's head was beginning to throb. This was complicated and he was getting it wrong. What else had he overlooked?

There was something else, something he'd forgotten, something important. The harder he tried to remember, the more uncertain he felt.

He'd have to go back inside and clean Danny's rifle, then decide whether to leave both weapons on the floor or put them back against the wall. Maybe he'd see it then, see what else was out of place.

His Nikes were still jammed in his shorts pockets and his socks almost dry on his feet. It took him only seconds to go to the kitchen sink, take a tea towel and don the rubber gloves again. He picked up Alec's rifle and leaned

111

it against the wall. As he bent to pick up Danny's rifle, the dogs set up a howling bark in the shed.

Dan tensed.

He knew that bark. It meant a vehicle was approaching. But it was too soon for anyone from town to get here and he couldn't hear a vehicle, so it must be some distance away. Maybe it was on the road. But the dogs shouldn't have heard it from here.

What was happening?

CHAPTER NINE

With the rifle still in his hands, he went outside and looked up towards the track. All was darkness. If a vehicle was approaching, then it hadn't reached the crest of the hill yet and he still had time to get away. He held his breath and listened carefully.

At first he didn't hear anything other than a slight crunching sound which he couldn't quite make out. Then suddenly, headlights blazed in his eyes and he heard a man's voice cry out, "There he is! The bastard's still there!"

"I see him, Dad!"

"Get him, Dad!"

It was Mr Perry and his two teenage sons.

Fear rose in Dan's throat as he turned and ran back inside. This was not in the script. No one had ever mentioned that the neighbours had come to the house, but of course it was logical. Mrs Perry probably took Connie into town and Mr Perry rushed to the Campbell's place to see if anything could be done for Alec. His boys were big strong lads and would not have let their father come alone. Even as he thought it, Dan wondered why he hadn't considered it before.

He dropped the rifle on the floor and took off up the passage at a run. Footsteps clattered up the veranda steps, then paused.

"Where'd he go?" he heard behind him. Then, as he opened the back door, "He's in the house! Get after him!"

"But he's got a gun, Dad!"

"So do we!" A shot was fired into the air. "Do you hear that, you bastard? You can't get far!"

Footsteps thundered onto the veranda as Dan closed the back door behind him. Where could he go? There were three of them and they were armed.

"Oh christ oh jesus oh no!" The Perry's had seen Alec's body. There was sudden silence from within the house. Dan froze on the back veranda. In that instant, he knew he only had one chance at escape. He had to trick them into thinking that he had run out into the darkness.

The wood box was next to him. It was waist high and sturdily built. He leapt onto it, his hands still swathed in rubber gloves, grabbed onto the guttering above his head and heaved himself onto the roof. Twisting around, he flattened himself so that he could see the veranda below him.

Dan heard retching coming from the front veranda, then the back door was flung open. Mr Perry turned on the outside light and leapt from the veranda, his rifle raised before him. "Where are you, you bastard?" he called into the darkness, firing another shot for good measure. "You can't escape!" As he said it, the sound of another vehicle cut through the night. Mr Perry ran back through the house. "Who's that?" he called out to his sons.

"It's the Murphys, Dad! And the Shanks!"

Two vehicles slid to a stop in the mud. Mr Murphy called out, "Your missus was worried about you. She stopped on her way into town to tell us what happened. I got the Shank boys here too. I saw what the bastard did to Connie. Where's Alec?" Then, "Holymotherofgod! What are we dealing with here?"

"The bastard's still here. He's gone out through the back of the house. He's got a rifle with him."

"If he did that to Alec, then he could do it to us. He could pick us off from out there. We gotta wait until the police get here."

"No! That'll be hours. We've got torches, we gotta get him while he's still close."

"Don't be bloody mad. Look what he did to Alec. That's no ordinary man out there. That's an evil bloody maniac."

The three men began to argue. Then Dan heard one of the sons say, "What's that smell, Dad?"

"What smell?"

"Sort of like laundry stuff, you know."

They paused and looked around them. Mr Shank said, "Christalmighty, he was cleaning up the place. Look, there's the mop outside, and the place smells like disinfectant. He came back to clean up after himself."

"You mean he walked around Alec like he wasn't there? Like he was doing the housework or something?"

"I never seen anything like this before. This bastard is a cold-blooded killer. I ain't going after a man like that in the dark. The police can do that."

"Yeah, maybe you're right."

"What if he comes back again?"

"Yeah. Alright, get the boys up here. Lock the back door. We stay here on the veranda until the police get here. Keep your guns at the ready. If you hear anything move, bloody shoot it!"

Dan heard them arranging themselves on the front veranda. They continued to discuss the situation between them.

The rubber gloves were slippery with sweat. He took them off and pushed them into the gutter, feeling an odd shape under his fingertips. It was a tennis ball caught amongst the leaves and debris. Mum had always been telling him off for throwing tennis balls onto the roof when he was a kid. He wrapped his hand around it and thought quickly.

He silently pushed himself into a sitting position and looked down. He'd only have one chance. In the glow of the back light, he saw that the top of the wood box was covered in years of blackened grime. It looked damp after the rain. He couldn't risk slipping in his socks, so he took the Nikes from his pockets and put them back on. Then he slowly stood, turned and threw the tennis ball hard.

It cleared the house and landed in the darkness a few yards from the front veranda with a heavy wet plop.

"What was that!" They were all on their feet in an instant. "Over there! Something's moving!" Two rifle shots. "No, over there!" More shots.

Dan dropped silently onto the wood box and leapt into the back garden amidst the chaotic noise coming from the other side of the house. He sprinted to the back paddock fence, hurdled it easily and kept running, leaving behind a perfect set of shoe prints on the grimy surface of the wood box.

The night closed in around him, damp and soft. Underfoot, the ground squelched around his shoes. He ran and ran and didn't stop until he looked back over his shoulder to see the houselights a mere pinprick in the distance. His heartbeat throbbed in his ears. Then he stopped to catch his breath and listen, poised to run again at the slightest sound.

Silence. Absolute muffled night silence. He felt like he was the only person left in the world.

Where the hell was he?

Looking around, he made out the solid shape of the distant hills against the night sky. The cloud cover was breaking up and a bright half moon outlined the clouds with silver edging. That wasn't good. A powerful pair of binoculars would spot his shape against the night sky from a long distance. He had to find cover.

New wheat shimmered like a misty grey sea in every direction. He knew the creek was somewhere between him and the hills.

He began to run again.

Find cover and hide. That's what he had to do. And then what? Get warm, for a start. Despite the sweat coming from every pore in his body as he ran hard, he was chilled to the bone, but he couldn't stay in one place for long. The police would bring tracker dogs. He was sure of that.

A line of low bush took shape ahead. The creek. Another few minutes and he'd be there. Then he could rest for a little while and take stock.

A breeze played at his heels. Dan wasn't aware of it at first, but it persisted. He looked behind him. He was alone. Then he became aware that the breeze was warm.

Warm and dry on this cold, damp night. It began to whip around his legs, chafing his skin. Rising to his waist, it played with his shirt, billowing it out around him. Then it was in his face and it was full of dust. Dust up his nose and in his eyes. He covered his nose and mouth and squinted his eyes against the onslaught. He began to cough and slowed to a walk.

The night brightened around him. At first he thought the clouds had parted and the half moon was lighting up the landscape, but a half moon wasn't this bright. Was it the police? Was it a police helicopter? Did they have such a thing out here thirty years ago? Looking up, he saw above him a cloudless sky lit up by a brilliant white full moon. He stopped.

The dampness had disappeared. As had the new wheat.

He was standing in a desert, a silver desert that stretched as far as he could see. The air was warm and dry.

He was back.

Dan burst into tears.

CHAPTER TEN

He stood and wept for a long time.

It was over. The nightmare/madness/time warp was over. He knew it as surely as he knew the sweat was drying on his body, as surely as the drought ravaged landscape sighed in the unforgiving breeze, as surely as the emptiness closed in around him.

Then he remembered Mum waiting at the hotel. It was the middle of the night. She would be frantic with worry by now. Had she called the police? Would they turn up to look for him as they had thirty years ago, but for very different reasons?

He had to get back.

There were no house lights to guide him back, but he knew the creek was just ahead. He started to run, but stopped quickly. The endorphin rush was over and he felt exhausted. It was an effort just to walk now. The line of lush bush growth that had led him from the road to the house just a few hours ago was revealed in the moonlight as a scattering of dead bushes and the skeletons of a few native trees. No water had flowed in these parts for many years.

Dan glanced at his wrist for the time. His watch was missing.

In that instant, he realised that was what he'd forgotten, what had been making him feel so uneasy. His watch. He'd given it to Alec in payment for the fuel. But that shouldn't matter, should it? He'd never heard his mother say anything about the stranger's watch. Perhaps the police hadn't found it.

His mind went one step further. It wasn't the watch that was the problem, it was the engraving on the back. Across the top were the words *Daniel James Campbell*, then underneath, *To Dad, Happy 40th, Love Hamish and Angus*, and the date under that.

It was a clue, a name, a link. Why hadn't he ever heard about the watch? It didn't make sense. Alec had pocketed the watch, it would have been found on his body.

It meant something, he knew that. As he laboured through the dust with the moon lighting his way, he tried to make sense of it all. For the past couple of hours, he'd not doubted for a minute that what he'd experienced was real. Not a dream or a nightmare or an hallucination. He felt the raw wound on his arm and winced with pain, felt the bareness and suddenly remembered the torn piece of shirt caught on the garden shed roof. He'd removed the shirt and forgotten the missing piece while he was cleaning up. He hadn't thought to retrieve it. But he didn't recall that ever being mentioned by the police either. Had they even found it?

No one had found the watch, he was sure of that, for if they had, they would have been searching for a man called Daniel James Campbell with two sons, Hamish and Angus, a man who turned forty a year ago. But the man had only ever been called The Stranger, nameless, with nothing known about him at all.

Dan's logical, analytical mind took over. There were pieces missing in this story and therefore only one possible explanation for the past few hours. He'd blacked out, hallucinated and wandered around in a dream-like state until he'd come to in the paddock here a few minutes ago. He'd obviously fallen at some stage, possibly getting through a fence, which would account for the wound on his arm, the torn sleeve and the missing watch. It all made sense. Didn't it? Please let it make sense!

It wasn't real. None of it had been real.

He wanted to cry again, but he was beyond tears now. He was dehydrated, his head was pounding and his body felt like it was failing him.

A light in the distance caught his attention. Was it the house? Was it happening again? His heart began to race and he felt paralysed. He couldn't take any more. He sank to his knees.

The light seemed to be moving from side to side and coming towards him. Perhaps it was the police looking for him, but in which time? Was he the stranger or was he Dan Campbell looking for his past?

The stranger. He wasn't the stranger. The stranger had happened thirty years ago, not a few hours ago. It had all been his imagination, born out of thirty years of grief and depression.

As the light got closer he heard a motor and a dog barking. A voice cried out, "There he is!" and he was suddenly caught in the beam of a spotlight just as he'd been in his hallucination barely an hour ago. The voice cried out again, "Is that you, Dan Campbell?"

Dan raised his arm weakly to acknowledge the question and awaited his fate. He felt a softness brush against him as the dog reached him first.

A dusty Landcruiser pulled up next to him and a tall grey-haired man got out. "Jason, get the water. He looks pretty crook." Dan felt a bottle of cool water held to his lips and gulped greedily. "Easy, mate, you don't want to bring it straight up again." A pair of strong arms supported him.

A second man chuckled with relief. "Christ, we could have been driving around all night looking for you. Good girl," he said, making a fuss of the dog, "good girl for finding him." He held a torch to Dan's face. "You're a sight for sore eyes, you are. Here, swallow this, it's a salt tablet, it'll help. We've got some tucker in the car, but you need a bit of fluid first. Looks like you've been through a bit, mate. We found your hire car by the gate and figured you got yourself lost. How'd you get that?" Dan felt a touch on his wounded arm.

"Fell getting through a fence."

"Yeah, it's pretty treacherous out here now. I'm Jason Perry. This is my father-in-law, John. My mother-in-law, Irene, asked us to come out to look for you. Seems your mother is in a bit of a state."

Dan looked up into the shadowed face. "Is she alright?"

"She was worried, mate. She figured you might have got yourself lost. After all, it's been thirty years since you were out here last and it's changed a bit, wouldn't you say?"

Dan nodded.

"We've got a satellite phone in the car. I'll call the pub and let Irene know we found you." Jason climbed into the driver's seat.

John squatted in front of Dan. "Can you get up, mate? Can you get in the car? Come on, take my hand. That's it. Up you go, into the front. Irene packed some food for you, some sandwiches and bananas. That's it, small bites at first. Here, have some more water. OK. That's good. Jason, everything alright at home?"

"Yeah. Irene's going up to Connie's room to tell her. Says she'll take her some dinner, too, she hasn't eaten since breakfast."

Dan let it all happen around him. It hadn't been real, none of it. This was real. He felt the tension and fear flow away from him.

"OK, mate, let's get you back to your mother. Mother's are special people, can't keep them waiting, hey, John?"

"Too bloody right." There was a moment of silence as the car bounced along the dusty paddock, it's barrenness even more stark in the headlights. Jason navigated carefully between the fence posts where they had cut the fencing wire to get onto the property. When they reached the hire car, Jason said, "You drive it back, John. I saw the keys in the ignition. I'll take Dan back in the Landcruiser."

The dog followed John. Jason waited until the hire car was in front of them and followed the dusty red glow of the tail lights.

Dan felt something was needed from him. "Thanks for coming out. I don't know what I would have done if you hadn't found me."

"I reckon you would have found your way back eventually. In the morning, you know, when you could get your bearings. It wouldn't have been so confusing then. Trouble is, there aren't any landmarks out here to guide you any more, not with the trees gone and all." Jason glanced briefly across at Dan's pinched, exhausted face in the dim light. "Gotta say, though, it's a bloody relief to see you're alright. We were getting real worried. We've been out here looking for several hours."

"I'm sorry to put you to so much trouble."

"It's no trouble, mate. Not for one of our own."

"One of our own?"

"Yeah." Jason chuckled. "You don't remember me, do you, Danny?"

Dan tried to pull his fuzzy thoughts into focus. There was certainly something familiar about this man. "I'm sorry, you told me your name, but I wasn't paying attention."

"Jason Perry." He paused until he saw recognition in Dan's face. "We used to go on the same school bus. I'm a few years older than you, so we didn't have too much to do with each other, but I remember you well."

"I remember you, Jason. You have a brother?"

"That's right, Barry. He's a city bloke now, went to Sydney to get work, doing alright for himself."

"What about the rest of your family. You were the next neighbours on from the Taylors, if I remember."

"Yeah, that's right. Mum and Dad both gone now. I moved my family into town about ten years ago. We help John and Irene with the pub. Couldn't stay on the farm. Christ, what farm? Look at it out here, bloody breaks my heart it does. It'll never recover, it's just desert now."

124

"I remember you at our farewell, before we left for England."

"Yeah, bit of a sad night, that was." Jason paused. "They never got the bastard, did they?" For a second, Dan looked confused. "Sorry, Danny. I didn't mean to … hell, it must have been rough for you and your mother."

"It's alright," Dan said quickly. "I'm alright. Mum's alright. We have made good lives for ourselves. It was a long time ago. No, they never found him." He paused, wanting to put this old neighbour at ease, then asked, "Do you remember much about that time?"

"Christ. I'll never forget it as long as I live. Still go over it my mind sometimes, wondering if I'd missed something that I could have given the police, thinking maybe it was my fault I didn't pay more attention to what I saw."

Dan's thoughts suddenly came into sharp focus. He shifted in his seat so that he could see Jason's face. "What do you mean? What did you see?"

"Him. I saw him, clear as a bell, standing not three yards away. You didn't know?"

"No. Nobody ever told me anyone saw him. I thought Mum and I were the only ones."

"I'm not surprised nobody told you. You went through a bad time back then. Losing your father that way, seeing your mother knocked around like that. And you were just a little kid. We all felt pretty sorry for you both. I guess someone thought you didn't need to know more than you already did."

The implications of what Jason was saying began to sink in. "Tell me, please. Tell me everything."

"You sure you want to know?"

"Yes. I need to know."

"Yeah, I reckon I'd need to know if I was you. OK." Jason slowed a little as he rounded a bend. The taillights ahead were drawing away, leaving them enclosed in a dusty bubble.

"Well, first we knew about it was when your station wagon turned up. Mrs. Averill – Connie – it must have taken every last bit of her strength to get to our place. We heard the horn and went outside and there she was, almost collapsed. Dad had to open the door and put his foot on the brake to stop the car from rolling or it would have ended up on our front veranda. She was … her face … well, I'd never seen anything like it. She was a mess. Lost a lot of blood. Mum put a tourniquet on her arm, then we wrapped her in lots of blankets and put you both in our car. Couldn't wake you up. Connie said she'd given you a sleeping tablet. Mum said that was a blessing, to leave you, it was better you didn't remember any of this. Dad kept saying, Where's Alec? Where's Alec? Then Connie said he was dead, he'd been shot by some bloke she didn't know. Dad got us boys and we took off like speed demons. Mum took off for town in the other direction. We were a good hour out of town, no phone lines out here back then. We were all pretty scared. First, we didn't know if your mother would make it, and second, we didn't know what we'd find when we got to your place." Jason glanced at Dan. "You alright with this, mate?"

Dan took a deep, slow breath. "Go on."

"Well, we got to your gate and Dad turned off the lights. Said it was best if we weren't seen coming. So we get to the top of the hill just before your house and we could see the lights on and someone moving around inside. Dad said, He's still there, get your guns ready. We'd been spotlighting the night before and our rifles were still under the seat. We loaded them, turned off the motor and rolled down to the house. Christ, I was terrified. Just before we got to the house, Dad turned the headlights on and there he was. Standing in the doorway, brazen as can be, with a rifle held across his chest."

Dan began to sweat. This was his hallucination being told in detail by someone else. "You got a good look at him?"

"Bloody oath. We all did. Big bastard, six four, six five …"

Dan thought, They were below me looking up, I would have looked taller than my six feet.

"… big across the shoulders …"

Yes, I'm broad shouldered.

"… and massive across the hips …"

Massive across the hips? What was he talking about? My hips? Of course. I had my Nikes shoved into the side pockets of my shorts. My hips would have looked much wider than normal.

"… huge hands …"

I was wearing rubber gloves.

"… wore those hippy clothes, you know, board shorts or something …"

Cargo shorts coming to just below the knees. Baggy, big expandable pockets, a garment not to be seen for another fifteen years.

"… white tennis shoes …"

Socks. I was in my white summer sports socks that come to just below the ankle. Another piece of clothing not around thirty years ago.

"... straight, sort of greasy lank hair ... black as the ace of spades ..."

My hair is wavy brown, but it was wet from the rain.

"... and arrogant. Glaring at us like he should have been there and we shouldn't have been."

Not arrogant. Shocked and afraid. And it was my home, that's why I looked like I belonged.

Dan asked anxiously, "His face? Did you see his face?"

"Yeah. I'll never forget his face as long as I live. White, you know, sort of pasty ..."

Not white, but drained of colour by fear and blanched in the intensity of the lights.

"... big black eyes ..."

Brown, but wide with shock and pupils dilated in the glare of the headlights.

"... small mouth ..."

Mouth pinched with fear.

"... a mean face."

Not mean, just scared and confused.

Dan was almost too afraid to ask, but he had to know. "You'd know him again if you saw him?"

"In a bloody instant."

But I'm here now and you don't see me.

Jason swung the wheel as they rounded a bend. "Been looking for the bastard ever since that day. Me and the wife, we've been on holidays from one end of Australia to the other and I been looking for him everywhere I go. Of course, he'd be an old man by now. I reckon he was in his late thirties, maybe early forties back then, he'd be seventy or so by now. But I'd know him. And if I ever did see him again, he be a dead man, for sure."

Jason was sitting beside the man he was sure he'd know under any circumstances and Dan was as safe as he ever could be. This was insane. "What happened then, Jason?"

"He bolted - went back inside the house. Then we heard the back door slam and Dad took off after him. Me and Barry ... well ... when we saw your father, we couldn't move. Dad came back, said he'd lost him outside somewhere. Then the Murphys and the Shanks turned up, said Mum had stopped long enough to yell out what had happened. She was scared for us, wanted them to back us up. There were ten of us, all armed and scared shitless. Dad told us to stay together cos the bastard was a cold blooded killer and he didn't want anyone else hurt. So we gathered on the veranda to wait for the police, but after a moment, we heard the bastard around the front. He'd circled around and was trying to pick us off. We fired a few rounds, but I don't know if we hit him. Then it went quiet, but we were too afraid to move from the veranda. He could have been anywhere. It seemed like hours before the police got there. They couldn't do much until daybreak, then they started the search. Coppers came from all over the state. Brought in sniffer dogs and all, but the trail went nowhere. Reckon the rain made it impossible to get his scent. Anyway, he was long gone. I've always thought he had a vehicle up the road somewhere, got away easy. There were a few reported sightings over the years, but nothing ever came of it."

Dan was silent. Jason, uncertain what the silence meant, continued. "I reckon you and Connie made the right decision, going to England and all. Things got pretty bad out here, lot of folks lost everything. We were luckier than most, we had the pub to fall back on, but even that's a bit of a struggle at times. I hear Connie's married again. Everything good there?"

"Yes, everything's very good there. My stepfather is a wonderful man. We've been very fortunate."

"I've been lucky, too. Married, couple of good kids." Jason went on to talk about his wife and children, about people Dan knew as a boy, about their teachers and local identities. He made it very easy for Dan to sit quietly and think about what he would say to his mother.

CHAPTER ELEVEN

By the time they got back to the pub, the dash clock showed it to be after 3.00 am. John was waiting for them downstairs. "Irene said Connie hasn't slept. She's upstairs in her room, Dan. She's been quite anxious, done a lot of crying. Reckon it's been tough on her. She's waiting for you."

Dan thanked the two men again and went upstairs, the trembling returning unexpectedly to make him feel weak and unsteady on his feet as he approached Connie's room. It had seemed so real, but it couldn't have been. Could it? None of it was possible. Was it? Even Jason's story could be explained. Perhaps as a boy, Dan had overheard someone speaking of the encounter with the stranger and that had slipped into his unconscious memory, only to surface during the dream/hallucination/madness.

One thing he was sure of right now was that he was awake, that everything around him was solid and real. Despite his fatigue and confusion, he had never been more certain of this moment of reality, for in the next few seconds, his mother's first response to his return would tell him what the truth was.

What would she say? Would she say it was him thirty years ago and that he'd somehow travelled back through time? Then that would be an admission that she'd murdered his father. He couldn't believe she'd ever have been capable of such an act, not the gentle mother he'd grown up with and believed he knew so well. Would she re-affirm that it was a stranger who'd committed the murder, as he'd always believed? That he'd had a nervous breakdown out there in the dust and heat, that this had been coming for the last thirty years because he'd never come to terms with his father's death? Or would she say it had been an hallucination brought on by heatstroke?

As he opened the door, Connie jumped up from the bed and turned towards him, her face pinched and pale, terror filled eyes red and swollen from prolonged weeping. His heart squeezed at the sight of her. She was clutching something fearfully to her chest. As he drew close to her, she suddenly thrust her hand forward and wordlessly gave him a brown paper bag.

This was not what he had expected.

Dropping into a chair, his eyes scratchy with fatigue, he said in a voice hoarse with emotion. "What's this?" He opened the bag. Inside were four faded colour photos, an old watch and a piece of stained fabric. He took the photos out.

Connie was watching him as if he might pounce on her. He couldn't stand it. "It's OK, Mum. I'm OK. Please, dearest, sit down. We're both exhausted."

She nodded and obeyed, perching anxiously on the edge of the bed, her hands folded in her lap like a school girl. He'd never seen his mother like this. He couldn't imagine what was going through her mind.

Turning his attention to the photos, he gasped. Connie jumped. "Mum, relax, everything's alright." He leaned across to take her hand comfortingly. She was cold, even though the room was very warm.

He looked back at the photos. They were yellowed around the edges and scrunched as if they'd been handled often. Obviously taken at night with a poor flash, the pictures showed faces turned pale against a black background. Even so, there was no mistaking their content.

The first photo was of himself as he was now with a young Connie. The second photo was of a pale and startled Connie. The third photo was of a sleeping boy on a veranda. The last photo was of himself squatting between Connie and the boy.

Da looked up, feeling stunned and speechless. He didn't know what to say.

Connie saw his confusion. "You told me to go back for the film. Remember?"

"Yes, but …"

"You told me," she repeated.

"And you did?"

"Yes," she whispered and continued in a hesitant voice. "I went back on my own just before we left for England. Some of the neighbours had been in to clean up the house and pack up for us. We were staying with the Taylors then. I think I'd forgotten about the film until the letter came from England and the Taylors made me an offer on the farm. Then I remembered you had told me that would happen and I remembered the film. I didn't know what to make of it all, but I began to worry about someone else finding the film. I told the Taylors that something had been missed, a tin of secret treasures that you kept under the floorboards in your bedroom. I wanted to go back for it."

"You knew about that?"

"Of course, Danny love. I'd always known. You left scratch marks where you used the screwdriver to lever the boards up. I found the marks when I was cleaning the floors."

"Oh Mum."

"I was scared that someone might have found the film when they were packing up, but it was still there. After all, it was months since…" She looked down quickly and Dan suddenly understood her fear.

She was afraid he hated her now. Afraid he blamed her. "So it was real, Mum?"

She nodded slightly, her eyes still wide with trepidation.

He cried, "I don't understand any of this!"

"Neither do I."

They stared at each other, unable to comprehend what they both now knew to be the truth. For the moment, it was too hard. Dan needed a distraction, so he turned his attention to the old watch. The liquid crystal display had long since faded and the back was corroded with moisture. Scratching at the corrosion, he saw letters appear. It was an inscription. He looked up. "Where did you find it?"

"The Taylors went back to the house when they first got back from the coast to get some things for us while we were still in hospital, and to bring the dogs back to their place. They found this around Lucky's neck, like a collar. They weren't sure what it was because there was nothing around like it at the time. The inscription on the back was muddied and barely legible, so I don't think they even noticed it. They thought it might have been a birthday present for you. I told them it was a novelty puppy collar

134

I'd found in a catalogue. I put it in my dressing gown pocket. I didn't tell anyone else about it. I remember Alec putting it in his overalls after you gave it to him on the veranda. How did it come to be around Lucky's neck?"

"Of course. I'd forgotten about that. Dad gave it to me when he came into the shed to get me for tea that night. Told me it was a worthless piece of junk and the stranger was a con man, that he couldn't make it do any of the things the stranger said it could do and that I could have it. I thought it was a great collar for Lucky. I'm surprised that the police hadn't found it."

"They might have looked around the shed, I don't know, but Lucky would have been snuggled up with her mother, so they wouldn't have seen it."

He looked down at the piece of stained fabric. "What's this?"

"After I found the film under the boot scraper, I thought I would take a walk around the garden to say goodbye, but I was only putting off going inside. It was the middle of winter and everything was looking bleak and bare. As I went past the garden shed, I noticed this lying on the ground behind the roses that grew next to the shed. I picked it up and knew immediately what it was. The police had missed it." Connie took the piece of fabric, leaned across and spread it over the upper part of Dan's arm. It fitted perfectly into the torn sleeve.

Dan gasped. "I tore the shirt when I jumped off the roof of the garden shed. It caught on the gutter. I didn't pay much attention at the time."

"No. There were other things that had your attention at that moment."

They were dancing around each other, afraid to say it openly.

Connie stammered on. "There was something else I found. When I lifted the floorboards to retrieve your treasure tin, I found a blackened, dried towel stuffed behind it. I knew what it was."

He nodded slowly. "What did you do with it?"

"I was afraid that someone living in the house later might find it, so I took it outside and buried it behind the shearing shed."

"Only I know about the towel under the floor. You couldn't have known because it happened after you had gone. Oh god, Mum, what is happening here? Have I lost it completely? This happened thirty years ago, but it was only last night for me. Christ, the stench of the kitchen is still in my nostrils, the smell of Dad, the sight of you after he'd beaten you, the contempt, the pure contempt he treated you with. It's burning my brain! And a few hours ago, I held a boy in my arms and that boy was me! I carried myself to the car. How can that be, how can any of it be? Is any of this real? Is my whole life an hallucination out of control? Will anything ever be normal again?" The tears burst from him.

Connie drew him to her side and held him tight, suddenly the mother with her little boy again. He sobbed into her, feeling her own release of tears wetting him. They were both shaking.

"I'm so sorry," she said. "I know you can never forgive me, I wish I hadn't done any of it, but …"

Dan sat up quickly and wiped at the tears. "It wasn't your fault, Mum. None of it was your fault. I heard him, I heard everything. He was going to keep you as a slave and get rid of me because I was nothing more than a pest to him." A blustering sob escaped him. "He was a monster, Mum! I know that now. You tried to protect me, you tried to keep the truth from me, but I know now. You were trapped. We were both trapped. What you did - you believed it was the only way to free us both. He would have killed you if you'd tried to leave again, like he killed your father. And he would have made my life hell, if he'd let me live that long. Oh Mum, Mum, I don't blame you. I blame him!"

"Oh Danny, if I had my time over again …"

"What would you have done? There weren't any women's refuges around back then. You were isolated, no one else knew, and you couldn't escape because he'd follow you. He would have killed you, Mum. It's happened to other women in that situation. He would have killed us both and found a way to get away with it. He didn't care who he hurt, he didn't have it in him to care. I mean, he raped you, for godsake. He raped you and kept working on the farm with Grandpa until he knew you were pregnant because he wanted the farm."

"Yes, but maybe I could have handled it differently."

He looked at his mother intently. "You could have got an abortion. Why didn't you?"

"It was suggested at the time, but I couldn't kill my own baby. You see, despite the circumstances of your conception, you were my baby and I was in love with you from the moment I knew I was pregnant. All I could think about from then on was how to protect you, how to care for you, how best to love you."

"And you did, Mum, more than I ever realised until now. I love you, Mum. You know I'd do anything for you, anything."

"I know, dearest, I've always known that, but for thirty years I've kept what I did a secret from you and it has been so hard, watching you grow up believing in something that I knew was a lie."

"You never let on, not once."

"You told me not to, remember?"

"How could I forget? I told you only last night." He put his hands up to his head. "Christ, I've got a headache you wouldn't believe."

"Me too."

Dan looked at her strained, exhausted face. "I've put you through a lot today, haven't I? I'm sorry Mum."

"You've nothing to be sorry for, dear boy. I've been to hell and back today, granted, but it was nothing compared to what you've been through. I've been so afraid for you."

"Afraid for me?"

"Of course. I knew where you were going, but I didn't know if you would ever come back. I thought you might get ... stuck, you know, not able to come back."

"I was frightened that would happen, too. I was frightened all the time. I'm still getting my head around it. A few hours ago, I was eleven years old and you were young and Dad was alive." Dan winced as he rubbed his temples. "I may never sleep again."

"Dearest, that's how I felt after it all happened. That's why I still take sleeping tablets to silence the demons in my head for a few hours, to give me some peace. You see, the horror of what I did has never left me, the guilt, the remorse. Surely there had to have been a better way back then, but I couldn't see it."

"I would have done the same thing if I had been in your circumstances, Mum."

"Do you really think that?"

"Yes, I really think that. Oohh, my head, it's going to explode."

Connie, ever the mother, rose and took something from her purse. They were her sleeping tablets. "I nearly killed you with these things thirty years ago. I have never gotten over that. But maybe tonight, a couple will do us both some good. And we'll talk some more in the morning. I've asked Irene not to disturb us. We both need to sleep. And then there is something I want to do."

Dan looked up at her. "Yes?"

"I want us to go back out there, to see what is really left of our old life on the farm. I need to do this, Danny. Can you bring yourself to go out there again?"

"Maybe I need to do it, too. To finish it."

"Yes, Danny love, let's finish it."

CHAPTER TWELVE

It was almost noon before Dan woke, his head heavy and his body aching. Connie was already downstairs. He showered, ate lightly and packed the car with food and drink.

As they drove out of town, Dan glanced at Connie's red puffy eyes. "I need to ask you something, Mum."

"Anything, love. I think we need to talk it through."

"I want to know if you ever told anyone. You know. About what really happened."

Connie was quiet for a moment before answering. "I told Terry before I married him. I risked losing him, I knew that, but I was so twisted up with guilt that I couldn't continue the relationship without him knowing the truth. When I told him that I had shot Alec, he wasn't as shocked or horrified as I expected. You see, Terry's sister was married to a violent alcoholic. You know the story. She left him, but not before she'd endured some terrible beatings and she's never really recovered. Suffers from depression, still needs medication to get through the day, as I do to get through the night. What you don't know, because it distresses Terry so much to talk about it, is that she tried to leave her husband when things first got bad and he came after her. Beat her terribly. She wouldn't press charges despite Terry's family urging her to do so because she was so afraid of him. She tried to commit

140

suicide not long after that and she came very close to succeeding. When she finally did manage to leave him, she lived in fear for years that he would come after her. She still does. Her nightmare isn't over. She won't be free until he's dead. So when I told him what our lives had really been like and what had driven me to do it, he just held me. Held me for a very long time."

"And what about me. Did you tell him it was me?"

"I told him everything. I showed him the photos. But Danny, I didn't really believe it was you at first. How could I? I didn't believe anything you told me that night because it was impossible. Then when the letter came from my aunt in England and the Taylors made me an offer on the farm ... well, I began to wonder. And then Terry walked into the pub one day and it brought it all back, what you'd said about him. Do you know that if you hadn't told me that I would meet him, that he was good and kind and that I would be happy with him, I wouldn't have given him the time of day. You see, after Alec, I never wanted a man near me again. I was a mess back then, Danny. Terry showed me a different way and I've never looked back. Then you brought Patricia home to meet me and her surname was Walsh and when Hamish was born, I understood where Hamish Walsh came from. I told Terry, I told him everything as it unfolded."

"What did Terry say?"

"He said that only time would give us the truth. As you grew, I saw the man in the photos begin to emerge. I didn't know what to think. Then one night, about four years ago when Terry and I were looking at the photos again, he said I should let it play itself out, be careful not to influence you in any way, not to sway you in any decisions you might make about going back. So I didn't. Then when you decided to come back and asked me to go with you … well, it's been a very emotional time for me."

"All these years, Mum, all these years you knew what would happen and you never said anything. It must have been very strange for you."

"At first, I didn't believe anything would happen. Then I began to wonder. And now I know." She was looking at him. "I just don't understand why."

"Neither do I. I don't understand any of it."

They drove on in silence.

When they arrived at the farm gates, Dan saw the gap in the fence nearby where the wires has been cut by Jason the night before and drove through onto the property. As they approached the crest of the hill, Connie shook her head sadly from side to side. "I don't recognise any of it/ It's like another planet."

As the house came into view, Dan gasped and Connie's eyes filled with unbidden tears.

Where once the house had been a graceful old lady surrounded by green trees and flower beds, there was now only decay and desolation in the midst of unrelenting barrenness. The roof had fallen in and the veranda collapsed at the front. The glassless windows had become dark sightless eyes. Not even a trace of the once glorious garden remained, the dusty treeless paddocks continuing as far as the eye could see. The sheds had long ago been raided for their sheets of iron and the equipment sold off. Nothing remained but the skeleton of the shearing shed in the back paddock, it's framework standing as tragic testament to another era.

Dan pulled up close to the house. "I can't believe it's come to this," he said sadly. "I was here only ... yesterday."

"Yesterday thirty years ago." Connie put a comforting hand on his arm, then murmured, "I could never have imagined ..." The sentence remained unfinished. No words could express what they both felt.

They left the car and walked around what remained of the house paddock, although there were no fences to guide them. "I remember three thousand white sheep against green spring grass, waiting there in the back paddock to be sheared, with the shearers coming out of their quarters over there," Connie pointed to an empty space near the remains of the shearing shed, "the sun barely colouring the sky, Mum in the kitchen cooking up a storm for them, Dad already getting the first sheep in, and me running around with the wool classer, learning the ropes." She sighed deeply. "They were good days, before Alec."

"I have good memories, too," Dan said, then added, "or at least, I think I do. How much of my memories were an illusion shaped by you, I'll never be sure of now. Do you want to look inside the house?"

Connie looked at the ruinous remains. "No, I don't think we'd find anything. No-one has lived out here for over twenty years. No, there's nothing in there I want to see again."

"Had enough then?"

"Yes. It's too dreadful. Let's go."

They turned away and trudged heavily through the dust to the car. Dan turned on the air conditioning and passed some biscuits and water to his mother, giving them a few minutes to steady their emotions while the interior of the car cooled. He looked at her. "OK?" She nodded.

As they drove away, Dan glanced at the house one last time in the rear vision mirror and felt it leaving him, rather than him leaving the house. He got to the crest of the hill and his breathing steadied. He heard his mother sigh. It was truly behind them now.

They were silent until they reached the gate pillars, and he remembered something. "I wonder ..." He stopped the car.

"What are you doing?"

"Yesterday — thirty years ago yesterday — I hid something inside this pillar. If it's still there, which is unlikely, it would be old like the photos and the watch and the piece of shirt sleeve you kept. I didn't know about those things you kept, but I know what I put here." He left the car and knelt next to what remained of the pillar, Connie coming up behind him to watch.

The apex of the pillar had crumbled away over the years and some of the stones had dislodged as the mortar had disintegrated with age, but the wide base was mostly intact. He'd used damp soil to replace the stone he'd removed, which would not have set like mortar. He saw a stone that sat lower than those around it. It came away easily and he peered inside. "Godalmighty. It's still here."

Connie stepped aside as he pulled the items from inside the pillar. A few remnants of plastic wrapping, shrivelled and blackened. Meaningless to anyone other than Dan who had placed them there intact just yesterday. Next came the plastic water bottle, opaque and brittle from heat and age. And there was something else. A long ragged piece of blackened cloth.

"What's that?" Connie asked.

"It's the bandage I took from your arm before you drove on to the Perry's house."

"I don't remember that."

"I do, because it was yesterday for me, but you were barely conscious at the time." He stared at the items for awhile, then said with calm wonder, "It really did happen, didn't it, Mum? I don't understand how or why, but it really happened. This is the final proof that I was really here, that I was the stranger."

Connie stroked the top of his head, feeling heat and sweat. "Yes, dearest. It's the final proof." She helped him to his feet and said thoughtfully, "Do you realise how much of our lives has been shaped by what you told me to do that night? I've always wondered what I would have done if you hadn't said any of those things. You know, about selling the farm and going to England and meeting Terry and making you believe your childhood was something it wasn't. Would I have made the same decisions?"

"What do you think?"

She stared off into the hazy distance. "I would have gone to England, but not because you said it would work out. Guilt would have made me go."

"I don't understand."

"Well, after that night, everyone around here was so kind and supportive, they couldn't do enough for us. Neighbours took over the farm and cleaned up the house after Alec's body was removed. People from all over came to visit me at the Taylors with such compassion, such goodwill, and all the time I was lying, pretending to be the grieving widow when I knew I had killed him myself. It was unbearable, so when the letter from my aunt came and the Taylors offered to buy the farm, I jumped at the chance to escape. It was another act of cowardice on my part."

"Cowardice? There is nothing cowardly about you, Mum."

"You don't think so? I murdered your father, Danny. Nothing could be more cowardly than that."

Dan took her by the shoulders and looked down at her intently. "Tell me something, Mum. What were you thinking at that moment when you pulled the trigger? What went through your mind? Do you remember?"

"How could I forget? There was only one thought in my mind at that moment. I thought you were lying dead in your bed and I longed to hold you in my arms, to join you in death, to never be separated from you again. I was crying out in my heart for you, crying out to be with you, to be with you in sweet, peaceful death. Oh god Danny."

Dan said earnestly, "Do you know what I was thinking just before I went from the present to the past? I was thinking, I want it back, I want my childhood back. Let me be a boy again with my Mum looking out for me. I wanted to feel your arms around me again like it was when I was a boy."

"What are you saying?"

"I'm saying you were longing for me, Mum, just as I was longing for you. We heard each other through time, don't you see?"

"Yes ... but how?"

"I don't know the mechanics of it. We'll never know, but it happened." Dan wiped sweat from his face. "Damn, it's unbearable out here. I need some cool air."

They went back to the air-conditioned comfort of the car and sat quietly while they recovered from the heat. As Dan was about to put the car into gear, Connie rested her hand on his. "Wait a minute, Danny. There's something I want to ask you."

Dan sat back and turned to her. "What is it, Mum?"

She paused. "Are you going to tell Trish and the boys?"

"About the stranger being me?"

Fear had returned to Connie's eyes. "About me."

"I hadn't thought that far ahead." Dan cast a long, slow look at the seared landscape around him. "You know, Mum, what happened here is in the past. Nothing can change it. You've kept a terrible secret in order to protect me, to give me a life I couldn't have had if you'd been locked up in jail. But all this time, your own life has been like a prison term for you, hasn't it? The guilt and fear, the lying. That must have been hard for you, because it's not in your nature to lie. I know that." He looked down at her. "Now I know the truth, and I'll protect you the way you protected me, so that you can continue to have the life you always should have had, but without fear. And without guilt, Mum, because I don't blame you. I blame Dad. He pushed you too far until you truly believed there was no other way out. Under the same circumstances, I would have done what you did, I'm sure of it. But I will tell Trish. I have to. You see, she knew you were keeping something from us. Her instincts have always been good about that sort of thing. She'll know if I'm keeping something from her. I can't treat her as an outsider, Mum, I love her too much. She should know, too."

Connie looked away. "Will she believe you?"

"What she'll make of our story, I can't predict, but I know she won't betray you. You don't need to worry. I know my wife. I'm as sure of Trish as you are of Terry. We're a family, a very close family, and we won't let anything damage that, not ever."

"And the boys? Will you tell them?"

He answered thoughtfully. "No. They don't need to know. Let them make their own destinies without the past to complicate their lives."

Connie took a deep breath. "Yes. You mustn't tell the boys."

"You know something, Mum? We can make our own destinies as well now. The horror of that day has bound your life and mine for thirty years, but it's over, it's finally over." He slipped the car into gear. "There's nothing here for us now. We're free of the past. The future is ours to shape as we wish. I want nothing more than to be at home. I think we should go back to town, see if we can change our flight to an earlier one, collect our luggage and go. What do you think?"

"Yes. Yes, indeed. I'm exhausted but I know I won't sleep properly until we get home."

"Oh, and there's something else." He smiled at her with a twinkle in his eye that she hadn't seen for a long time. "For the first time in forty years, you've forgotten what day it is."

Connie gave him a perplexed look, then returned the smile. "How could I forget that? Happy birthday, darling boy, happy birthday."

THE END

DAMAGED GOODS
By C. A. HOCKING

A Gripping Gothic Saga
of Abuse, Revenge and Love

Damaged Goods is a gripping gothic saga about three young sisters trapped in a childhood of unrelenting abuse at the hands of their cruel father. In order to survive their nightmare, Helen, Sis and Sweetypie create a secret world for themselves where their love for each other sustains them.

But children grow up and the day comes when the sisters know they must end their torment, whatever it takes. They plot a brutal revenge on their father, but not all goes as planned and Helen flees her family home and her beloved sisters.

Fifty years after leaving, Helen returns to find Sis and Sweetypie much as she had left them. Or so it seems at first, until she discovers secrets within secrets and an act of vengeance that still haunts their lives. So begins a journey for each of them that will ultimately end in tragedy, closure and release.

HOME TO ROOST
By C. A. HOCKING

A Powerful Drama of Betrayal, Abandonment and Redemption

Was Marian born evil, or did life make her that way?

Australian Prime Minister Marian Hardwick has achieved everything she ever desired to become the most powerful woman in the country. She is admired by some, but seen as ruthless, calculating and manipulative by others.

Only two men really know her – her husband and her brother – but one loves her and the other hates her. When one threatens to destroy her by revealing a secret buried deep in her past, the other can save her, but first he must break her completely.

Marian's life unravels as everything she ever believed in is exposed as a lie. If she is to survive, she must confront the greatest challenge of all – the truth about herself.

SARAH ANN ELLIOT
Book 1: 1823-1829
By C. A. HOCKING

An Epic Family Saga based on a true story.

Sarah Ann Elliott was born in 1823 into a family of weavers whose lives were entirely dependent on the textile mills of the booming Northern England town of Stockport.

Her family is much like any other with highs and lows, joys and sorrows, but when 10,000 spinners and weavers go on strike for nine months in the infamous 1829 Stockport Turnout, the Elliotts are plunged into a life of hardship and turmoil from which no one is spared.

Little Sarah Ann is swept along with the events that surround her and it is only the love of her family and her indomitable spirit that will carry her through.

Sarah Ann Elliott Book 1 is a poignant and harrowing story of one family's struggle to survive the grim mill towns of 19th century England, and is the first book in The Sarah Ann Elliott Series

OLD FARTS ON A BUS
By C. A. HOCKING

What happens when you put 30 eccentric senior citizens who don't know each other on a bus in a foreign country?

Quite a lot actually. And it's more fun than a barrel of monkeys!

Old Farts On A Bus is an insightful, humorous and sometimes poignant look at the challenges and eccentricities of growing older.

AUNT EDNA and the Lightning Rock
By C. A. HOCKING
Book 1 of the AUNT EDNA Stories

When Aunt Edna learns that her 11 year-old orphaned niece, Isobel is coming to live with her, she has a panic attack. Goodness, whatever will she do with a niece? After all, Aunt Edna is an Eternal with magical powers and Isobel is a Mere Mortal.

And what will Diggidydog, Grumblebumkin, The Great Smoking Beastie and Barking Wood Stove make of a niece? Not to mention the five Ghosts on the veranda and Frozen Bert in the freezer.

An Australian Children's Fable
of Weirdness and Wonder!

Made in United States
Troutdale, OR
03/16/2025